"An affirmation of friendship   whodunit, *The Whole Cat and Caboodle* marks a promising start to a series sure to appeal to anyone who loves a combination of felonies and felines."   —*Richmond Times-Dispatch*

"Ryan kicks off the new Second Chance Cat Mystery series with a lot of excitement. Her small Maine town is filled with unique characters. . . . This tale is enjoyable from beginning to end; readers will look forward to more."
—*RT Book Reviews*

"If you enjoy a cozy mystery featuring a lovable protagonist with a bevy of staunch friends, a shop you'd love to explore, plenty of suspects, and a supersmart cat, you'll love *The Whole Cat and Caboodle*."   —*MyShelf.com*

"I am absolutely crazy about this series. . . . The cast of characters is phenomenal. . . . I loved every minute of this book."   —*Melissa's Mochas, Mysteries & Meows*

"If you enjoy a lighthearted mystery; a smart, cute cat; and [a] wonderful heroine, then I suggest you read this series."
—*The Reading Cafe*

"If you are looking for a charming cozy mystery with a smart main character and an adorable cat, then you should check out *The Fast and the Furriest*."   —*The Avid Reader*

CaT GoT YoUr KiLLEr

A SECOND CHANCE CAT MYSTERY

Sofie Ryan

BERKLEY PRIME CRIME
New York

BERKLEY PRIME CRIME
Published by Berkley
An imprint of Penguin Random House LLC
1745 Broadway, New York, NY 10019
penguinrandomhouse.com

ISBN: 9780593550267

First Edition: March 2025

Printed in the United States of America
1   3   5   7   9   10   8   6   4   2

The authorized representative in the EU for product safety and compliance
is Penguin Random House Ireland, Morrison Chambers, 32 Nassau Street,
Dublin D02 YH68, Ireland, https://eu-contact.penguin.ie.

For Fran, who always believed in me.
"And flights of angels sing thee to thy rest."

CAT GOT
YOUR KILLER

Chapter 1

Elvis *had* left the building, but he hadn't left the parking lot. He was sitting on the front passenger seat of Liz's new car and the two of them were engaged in a staredown. Seeing as how Elvis was a very confident black cat with a scar across his nose that only added to his rakish charm, and Liz was Elizabeth Emmerson Kiley French, CEO of the Emmerson Foundation, I knew it would probably take a while. Luckily, it was warm for late May in coastal Maine.

Liz wanted Elvis in the backseat on a flattened cardboard box that she had taken out of my recycling bin. The cat continued to calmly look at her, seemingly without blinking, and I had the sense that he thought Liz's idea was ridiculous so he wasn't going to dignify it with any response other than to stare at her until she relented.

Liz's granddaughter, Avery, stood by the front bumper of the car, arms crossed and a scowl on her face. She was deeply offended by the idea that Elvis should be sitting on a cardboard box on the backseat. Liz and Avery often butted heads, but they loved each other fiercely. They were very much alike, although both of them would have vehemently denied it.

"Nonna, cats are very clean in general and Elvis is in particular. He isn't going to get your new car dirty."

Liz's "new" car was a 1976 sable black Cadillac Fleetwood Brougham, bought from a collector who had spent more time lovingly caring for it than actually driving it.

Elvis just continued looking at Liz.

"That is neither here nor there," Liz said. "If you plan on eating supper anytime soon pick up that furball and put him on the backseat."

I knew that look in Avery's eyes. I'd known Liz all my life and I'd seen the same look on her face innumerable times. I'd seen it more than once from Avery, for that matter. "Not until you apologize to Elvis," Avery said, a flash of defiance in her eyes.

Liz's chin came up. "I am not apologizing to a cat," she said. To be fair, Liz didn't like apologizing to anyone.

Avery squared her shoulders. "Then it's going to be a long time until supper."

Avery had been living with her grandmother for several years now because she had a difficult relationship with her parents. She was about to graduate from her unconventional private school and had been accepted at Benton College, a small private college about forty minutes away, where she was going to major in physics and minor in art because she hadn't decided whether she wanted to be an astronaut or an artist.

Liz looked at me as I moved past her carrying a large cardboard box. "Do something," she said.

"I am doing something," I said. "I'm putting this box in my SUV."

"Well, stop doing that and come get this insolent animal of yours out of my new car."

I laughed. "And why should I do that? If you want Elvis out of your car then pick him up yourself."

"I might just do that," she said. "Or I might just leave him here to fend for himself all night."

She looked at Elvis again as though he could somehow understand her threat—which, given how smart he was, wasn't totally unlikely. The cat was unfazed.

"Threats don't work on Elvis," I said. "He lived on the street, remember? He's perfectly capable of taking care of himself."

Mr. P. came out of the shop then, his messenger bag over one shoulder. Alfred Peterson was pretty much the smartest person in the room no matter the company. He was also kind and humble and scarily skilled behind a computer keyboard. On top of all of his many other skills he was a private investigator, licensed by the state of Maine, a fact that often surprised people because he looked like a sweet little grandfather who played chess at the park. And as a matter of fact he did play chess, including at any given time, a couple of correspondence chess games by email with top chess players from all over the world.

Mr. P. walked over to the car, excusing himself as he made his way past Liz. He picked up Elvis from the front passenger seat, and then sat down on the backseat, on top of the piece of cardboard Liz had put there. He set his messenger bag at his feet and settled Elvis on his lap. The cat seemed to smile at Mr. P. and then went back to looking at Liz.

The old man smiled. "While I do concede I am stretching the definition of transitive property, I do believe that Elvis has now met your conditions for riding in your new car." He leaned forward to look over the front seat. "It is a splendid vehicle, one of Detroit's best, and you have, as always, impeccable taste." He turned to look at Avery. "Would you please go help Rose with her things?" he asked.

"Sure," she said. She gave him an admiring smile. Then she turned her attention to her grandmother. "Nonna, if Mr. P. is sitting on the cardboard and Elvis is sitting on Mr. P., then Elvis is sitting on the cardboard."

"If A equals B and B equals C, then A equals C," Liz said tartly "You don't have to explain Euclid to me."

Avery started for the back door. "Probably because he was one of your teachers," she muttered.

"I heard that," Liz retorted.

"That was the point of saying it out loud, Nonna," Avery said as the back door closed behind her.

I could see from the hint of a smile that pulled at the corners of her mouth that Liz wasn't really annoyed. She looked at Elvis, pointed one exquisitely manicured, lavender-tipped finger at him and said, "Don't think you've won."

The cat tipped his head to one side and almost

seemed to give Liz a smug smile. I had the feeling he was certain he'd won.

I put the box I'd been carrying on the backseat of my SUV, then walked over to Liz and put my arms around her shoulders, leaning my head against hers. Liz and my grandmother had been friends since they were girls. She was family. "Alfred is right," I said. "This is a fabulous car."

Liz shot me the side eye. "And you are not driving it."

"I'm a good driver," I said.

Liz gave a snort of derision. "You drive like your grandmother."

I raised my head and gave her a wide-eyed look of innocence. "You mean well and responsibly?"

"I mean like the devil himself is on your tail."

My grandmother was the one who had taught both me and my brother, Liam, how to drive and all three of us had been known to stretch the speed limit from time to time but I still maintained we were good drivers. I gave Liz my best wheedling look. "Please. Maybe just a couple of laps around the parking lot?"

"Maybe the twelfth of never," Liz said.

"Okay," I said. "Just one little lap around the parking lot."

"No."

"Can I just sit in the driver's seat?"

"No. And for the record, missy, I told your grandmother the same thing when she asked."

I leaned over and kissed Liz's cheek. "You're very

mean," I said. I headed for the back door. "But I'll wear you down. I always do."

She gave another snort of skepticism.

"Love you," I said. I waited for her usual response and after a moment it came. "Yeah, yeah, everybody does," she said.

I stepped inside the shop just as Mac was coming out, carrying a large box. Mac was second in command at Second Chance and first in my personal life. The box was filled with books from the Magic Treehouse series. I needed to go through them to see which books were there and what kind of shape they were in. I had purchased the books from Teresa Reynard, one of the pickers I bought from regularly for the shop, and given the luck I'd had with two boxes of Babysitter's Club books I had purchased from Teresa a month ago, I felt optimistic about selling these ones.

My shop, Second Chance, was a repurpose store, a place where everything from furniture to housewares to musical instruments to, yes, books—most items from the '50s through the '70s—got a second life. It was one part thrift store and one part secondhand shop. Some things even got new uses altogether, like the china cups and saucers that were now tiny planters or the maps that had been turned into lampshades.

Second Chance was located in an old brick house, built in the 1800s in North Harbor, Maine. "Where the hills touch the sea" was the way the town had been described for more than two hundred years. It stretched from the Atlantic Ocean up to the Swift Hills. Being on the ocean we were often battered by winter storms with piles of snow and bitterly cold temperatures.

The town had originally been settled in the 1760s by the Swift family. Its population more than tripled in the summer and early fall. North Harbor was full of history with beautiful old buildings, award-winning eateries and unique small businesses like Second Chance.

"Is there anything else besides this box?" Mac asked. He was tall and lean with dark skin and dark eyes. He wore his hair cropped close to his scalp.

"That's it," I said. "I just need to get my sweater and my bag and I'm ready."

"Is the Liz-slash-Elvis skirmish over?"

I nodded.

"Who won?"

"Who do you think?" I said.

He thought about the question for a moment, his mouth twisted to one side. "I'm going to give the edge to Elvis," he said.

"We have a winner," I said with a grin. "They're just getting ready to leave."

Liz was taking Avery, Rose and Mr. P. to Rose's apartment, where she was making supper for all of them. Elvis was going because Rose had invited him. Like Avery and Mr. P. she saw the cat as part of our rather eclectic family. We were very late leaving the shop thanks to two tour buses that had shown up just before closing time.

Rose and I were next-door neighbors because her apartment was in the house I owned, a restored

Victorian in a quiet downtown neighborhood. It was divided into three apartments. I lived in the ground-floor front unit. Rose had the apartment that looked out over the backyard. My grandmother, Isabel Grayson Scott, and her husband, John, lived on the second floor. The whole situation shouldn't have worked and most people got a look of mild horror on their faces when they heard about it, but the thing was, it did work. Neither Rose nor Gram were judgy people and I knew they would always take my side no matter what I did. Plus Rose kept me in cookies.

Mac and I weren't going for dinner, although we had been invited. We were headed across town to the garage where Mac had been working on building a small wooden boat for the past three months. The garage rental had been my Valentine's gift to him. Mac had wanted to build a wooden sailing dinghy for a long time. Memphis Guitard, the brother of Cleveland Guitard, another one of my pickers, had bought a house near the water at the far end of town. Memphis had been happy to rent the garage space for six months once he knew why I wanted it. I hadn't seen the boat-in-progress in over two weeks and I was eager to get a look at it. It made me happy to see how much Mac loved working on it.

Memphis was one of those people who had never come across an electronic device he couldn't figure out and he and Mr. P. had become fast friends after Cleveland had introduced them. That friendship sometimes made me a bit nervous because Mr. P.'s computer skills, and Memphis's facility with small electronic devices, left me half expecting to wake up someday and find out the two of them had quietly and benevolently taken over the world while the rest of us were all sleeping.

Rose and Avery came into the workroom. Avery was carrying one of Rose's canvas tote bags. I knew it held a large metal cake tin, two tablecloths with tea stains Rose insisted she could get out and a teddy bear she had decided needed a new sweater.

Rose smiled at me. "Have fun," she said. She gestured toward the shop over her shoulder. "We need to figure out a new window display some day this week."

"I have some ideas," Avery said, turning from the box of books she'd been looking inside.

"Good," Rose said. "I was hoping you would say that."

Avery smiled and headed out to the parking lot, holding the door for Mac.

"I assume that figuring out a window display is code for planning a grad party for Avery," I said.

Rose patted my arm. "You've always been quick on the uptake, sweet girl," she said. "I'll need your input on the cake."

"I'll force myself to help you with that because I'm a giver," I said solemnly.

Rose laughed.

I picked up my bag and my hoodie and we stepped outside. I stopped to lock the door.

"Let's go, Rose," Liz said. "We're burning daylight."

"We'll talk tomorrow," Rose said to me. She headed for the car, stopping to pat Elvis on the head and smile at Mr. P., who she called her gentleman friend because she thought boyfriend sounded silly at her age. She gave the car a long appraising look and then nodded her approval. "You have wonderful taste," she said to Liz. "This car is a classic."

Liz gave her a small smile. "Thank you," she said.

Avery was already in the back with Mr. P. and Elvis, and Rose slid onto the front passenger seat. "I feel a bit like a movie star," she said.

Liz walked around the front of the car and got in the driver's side. I watched them pull out of the parking lot and thought how much I wanted to drive that car.

Mac came up behind me and rested his chin on the top of my head. "She's not letting you drive that car, you know," he said.

I turned and looked up at him. "I can wear her down."

He shook his head and smiled. "I can see this is going to be entertaining if nothing else."

I made a face at him.

He laughed. "You ready?" he said.

I nodded. "Let's go."

We drove out to Memphis's property. It was a beautiful evening. The sun was going down and the sky was streaked with pink and red.

"Renting this space is the best gift anyone has ever given me," Mac said as we made the turn toward Memphis's house.

"So you're not disappointed that I didn't get you the Bob Ross Chia Pet for Valentine's Day?" I teased.

Mac held up his thumb and index finger about half an inch apart. "Maybe just a little bit."

"Christmas is only seven months away."

"Don't toy with me," he said.

We both laughed.

"Do you think you'll be done by the time the six months is up?" I asked.

He nodded. "I hope so, but Memphis has already said I can have more time if I need it."

We parked in front of the big garage door. Mac unlocked the side door and we went inside. The space smelled like wood. The boat was in the middle of the space.

My eyes widened in surprise. "You finished the hull," I said.

He nodded and the pride was evident in his smile. "There's still a lot to do, but I feel like the most challenging part is over."

I walked around the boat. It was only ten feet long but it looked so much bigger in the small space of the garage. I ran a hand over the long planks of wood that made up the hull. I looked at Mac. "This is beautiful," I said.

"It's not a 1976 Cadillac Brougham," he said.

I smiled. "It's better, but don't tell Liz I said that."

"Are you going to want to take this out then?" He teased.

"Absolutely," I said. "If you'll teach me to sail."

"I will," Mac said.

Behind us there was a knock on the door. We both turned around to find Memphis standing there. "I didn't mean to interrupt," he said, "but is it okay if I have a peek?"

"Sure," Mac said.

Memphis came in and, like I had, slowly circled the hull. "Very nice," he said.

Memphis was a couple of inches shorter than his big brother, Cleveland. He was dressed in all black as he often was, his thick hair pulled back in a ponytail. He continued to move around the boat, no surprise because there always seemed to be a current of energy running through Memphis.

"Is Cleveland at the house?" I asked. "I noticed his truck when we pulled in."

"He's down on the beach," Memphis said, gesturing over his shoulder. "Something in the water caught his eye." He turned his attention back to the boat and asked Mac what he'd decided on for paint.

They started talking and I decided to go say hello to Cleveland. I knew Mac and Memphis would be a few minutes. Memphis had been very interested in the whole building process, even though he wasn't a sailor.

I walked across the back of the property and over to the edge of the embankment that dropped down to the water below. I could see Cleveland, who had waded out to his midthighs. I couldn't really see what he was after. It was caught in a mass of seaweed and blue plastic tarp.

I started down the path to the sand below. As I reached the beach I realized that it was a person floating in the water, tangled in the seaweed. My stomach lurched and I bolted down the sand toward Cleveland, who was just standing there. I splashed through the water to get to him.

I pulled at his arm. "C'mon, help me. We need to do CPR."

Cleveland shook his head. "It won't help," he said.

I looked at the body caught in the seaweed and realized that he was right. CPR wouldn't help. The person was dead.

Chapter 2

I felt in my pocket for my phone but Cleveland put a hand on my arm and shook his head. "I already did that," he said.

I realized he meant he had called nine-one-one. Cleveland, who was ex-Army and usually very competent, seemed a little rattled by finding the body. I wondered if this had triggered some old and painful memories.

Cleveland was a solitary person much of the time—very different from Memphis. He was taller than his younger brother and muscular with strong arms. I'd once seen him do pull-ups on a tree branch. His dark hair was shot with gray and there was a day's stubble on his face.

I could see that the body was going to drift out into deeper water if we didn't pull it in onto the sand. I knew we shouldn't be tampering with it but bringing it in seemed like a better idea than letting it keep floating away.

"We need to get the . . . the body out of the water," I said to Cleveland. "The tide is still coming in."

He nodded. "You take that side and I'll take this one," he said. Together we got the body far enough out of the water that the tide wouldn't be able to pull it back in again. It was cold, further proof that the person—it looked to be a man—had been dead for a while.

I bent down and pulled some tendrils of seaweed away from the man's face. Part of the ragged tarp had wrapped itself around most of his head. It felt disrespectful to leave it twisted around him like that, but I couldn't get it loose. "'And flights of angels sing thee to thy rest,'" I whispered, something I'd heard my grandmother say more than once when someone died.

The man didn't look like he had been in the water very long. Except for a gash on his head I couldn't see any injuries. It was almost as though he'd fallen asleep on the sand and the waves had just lifted him out into the water. As I straightened up, Cleveland looked at me and said, "Thank you."

I wasn't sure if he meant for the words or moving the seaweed. I wondered if he knew who the man was, but before I could ask, Cleveland gestured at the embankment. "One of us should go tell Memphis and Mac what's going on and wait for the police," he said.

I hesitated for a moment and when he didn't volunteer said, "I'll go."

Cleveland nodded but didn't say anything.

I climbed back up the path. Water oozed out of my shoes and dripped down from my jeans and the bottom of the T-shirt I was wearing. At some point before I'd gone in the water I'd yanked off my hoodie. I had no idea where it was now. I noticed a magenta canvas backpack on the sand at the edge of some seagrass. I wondered if it belonged to the dead man. Had he been taking pictures or maybe picking up shells or pieces of driftwood?

As I headed across the grass I could hear sirens. Mac and Memphis were standing by the side door of the garage. Mac smiled when he saw me. "Hey, I didn't know where you went," he said. Then he seemed to notice my wet clothes and disheveled appearance. The smile faded. "Are you all right?" he asked.

I nodded and looked at Memphis. "Cleveland is okay, too."

His dark eyes narrowed. "What happened?"

I tucked a clump of wet hair behind one ear. "He found a . . . body in the water. I, uh . . . I helped him pull it up onto the shore."

Memphis looked away and swore. Then he focused on me again. "Do you know who it is?"

"No," I said. "Whoever it was it doesn't seem like they were in the water very long."

The sirens were getting louder. Mac pulled off his own hoodie and wrapped it around me. Memphis gestured in the general direction of the water. "I should go and check . . ." He let the end of the sentence drift off.

I nodded. I didn't think it was good for Cleveland to be alone with the body.

Memphis headed across the grass and Mac wrapped me in his arms. "You're shaking," he said.

"The water was cold," I said.

"What happened?" he asked, one hand rubbing my back,

I shrugged. "I don't know. I walked over to the edge of the embankment and saw Cleveland standing in the water next to the body. I . . . I didn't know it was a body then."

"What do you mean, standing there?"

"I mean he wasn't doing anything. I think . . . I don't know . . . I think he may have been in shock."

Before I could say anything else the police and ambulance arrived. Mac showed them where to go. One of the paramedics noticed my wet clothes. "Are you okay?" she asked.

"I'm fine," I said. "I just waded into the water to help pull in the . . ." I didn't finish the sentence and she nodded her understanding.

"Get some dry clothes as soon as you can and maybe a cup of coffee," she said.

"Thanks, I will," I said. I stood for a moment watching her make her way to the top of the embankment and then I walked over to join Mac, who was standing at the top of the path. Below us I could see Cleveland talking to a police officer. Memphis was beside him.

"They're probably going to want to talk to you," Mac said.

"I know," I said.

We stood in silence for a couple of minutes. Then Mac said, "I don't understand. What happened?"

I pushed my hair out of my eyes but kept my gaze focused on what was happening on the beach below me. "I walked over here to see if I could see Cleveland. You and Memphis were talking and I hadn't seen Cleveland in days. You know he keeps an eye out for things I'm looking for. I wanted to tell him to add a couple of kitchen stools to the list. I saw him standing in the water but I couldn't see what was next to him."

I looked at Mac then. "I honestly thought he had found something worth saving. You know how Cleveland is. He finds things in the oddest places."

Mac nodded.

My stomach still felt as though it had tied itself into a knot. I folded my arms over my chest. "I started down the path to join him and see what it was. Partway down I realized it was a body floating in the water. I ran." I closed my eyes for a moment. "Once I got close enough I knew there wasn't anything that could be done for . . . whoever it was. That's why Cleveland was just standing there."

Mac put an arm around me and I leaned my head on his shoulder. "Cleveland said he had already called nine-one-one. The two of us pulled the . . . body in onto the shore because it was starting to drift out." I tucked my hands into my armpits. I was cold even with Mac's hooded sweatshirt wrapped around me and the warmth of his body next to me.

"Maybe it was a tourist who had been swimming," Mac said. I noticed how he avoided looking at the body down below us. Part of me wished I hadn't seen it, either.

I glanced back over my shoulder and saw that Michelle had arrived. I lifted a hand so she'd know I'd seen her and waited for her to join us. Michelle Andrews and I had been friends since we were kids. Back then I never would have expected her to become a police detective.

"What's going on?" she asked. She wore dark trousers with a blue shirt and a cropped navy blue jacket.

"Cleveland found a body," I said.

She looked at my wet clothes.

"I helped him get it out of the water."

"Was it a man or a woman?"

"Man," I said.

Michelle looked around. "What are you doing out here?" she said.

I pointed at the garage. "This is where Mac is working on his boat. The property belongs to Memphis Guitard. He and Mac were talking. I decided to go talk to Cleveland."

I knew Michelle would know Cleveland and Memphis were brothers. "Memphis had said Cleveland was down by the water because he'd noticed something and had gone to see what it was." I cleared my throat. "From up here I couldn't really make out what was floating down there. There was seaweed twisted all around . . . what was there."

Michelle nodded. "What did you do when you got down to the water?"

"Cleveland had called nine-one-one. I'm sorry, I know you're not supposed to touch anything in this kind of circumstance but we pulled the body up on the shore because it was drifting out into deeper water. Other than that we didn't touch anything. It was . . . it was too late for CPR."

"It's all right," Michelle said. She took a couple of

steps forward and looked to see what was happening down below us. Then she turned to me again. "I need you to stay around for a while, okay?"

"I can do that," I said.

Mac pointed at the garage. "We'll be there," he said.

Michelle smiled. "That's fine. Thanks." She put a hand on my shoulder for a moment. "Go find something dry to put on. I'll talk to you in a bit." She headed down the path.

It was almost dark now.

"Michelle's right," Mac said. "We need to find you something dry to wear. At least I have a coffee maker."

"I'm pretty sure I have an old, paint-spattered pair of jeans in a bag in your truck. I tossed them in the last time we went prowling around on recycling day in case I had to go through anything gross."

We walked back to Mac's truck and the bag was there with the jeans and an old pair of canvas shoes I'd forgotten I'd put in as well. I had no socks but the dry shoes were warmer than my wet sneakers. In dry clothes—including an old sweatshirt of Mac's that he had left in the garage—with my hands wrapped around a cup of coffee, I was much warmer. Mac pushed me to eat half a sandwich, and even though I didn't think I wanted it, once I ate it it felt better.

Memphis poked his head around the open door about twenty minutes later. "I just want to make sure you're okay," he said.

"I'm good, thanks," I said. "I have dry clothes and a cup of coffee." I leaned sideways to look past him. "Where's Cleveland?"

"He left," Memphis said. "He just . . . I think he needed some time by himself. You know how he is."

I nodded.

"How about a cup of coffee?" Mac said.

Memphis swiped a hand across his face. "Yeah, that sounds good. Thanks."

Mac grabbed a mug that I knew had come from a free box at a yard sale. He handed Memphis the coffee and gestured at the small carton of milk and Mason jar of sugar on the wooden tray table next to the mismatched kitchen chairs he had for seating.

Memphis took a long drink and wrapped his hands around the mug the way I had. He leaned against the wall instead of sitting down.

"Do they have any idea what happened?" I asked.

He shook his head. "I heard the paramedics say the body probably wasn't in the water very long."

"Do you think it was someone who got caught in a rip current and drowned?" Mac said.

Memphis shrugged. "It's possible."

I opened my mouth to say the dead man had been wearing jeans and a T-shirt, not a swimsuit, but I closed it again. People went out in the water all the time in their street clothes. It was a bad idea but they did it anyway. Maybe he had just waded out too far.

"This is private property," Memphis continued, "but it doesn't stop people from coming and swimming here. People trespass along the back as well. Seem to think it's some kind of public trail. If someone was walking too close to the edge . . ."

He didn't finish the sentence so I did, more thinking

out loud than anything else. "They could have fallen over and been pulled out when the tide came in."

Memphis took another drink of his coffee and nodded.

There was a knock on the door. I looked up. Michelle was standing there. "Hey," she said. "I just came to tell you that you can go now. I'll probably want to talk to you tomorrow, though."

"You know where to find me," I said.

She looked at Memphis. "I might have some questions for you tomorrow as well."

"I'll be here all morning," he said. "I'm setting up a security system in Rockport after lunch."

Michelle looked around. "Where's Cleveland?" she asked.

Memphis jerked his head in the direction of his house.

"That's fine," Michelle said. "There's no need for him to hang around, either." She pulled her phone out of the inside pocket of her jacket, looked at the screen for a moment and put it back again.

"Have either of you seen anyone around here lately?" She moved a finger between Memphis and Mac.

They both shook their heads.

"Okay," she said. "If you do remember anyone, let me know." She looked at me. "We'll talk tomorrow."

Michelle left and Memphis drank the last of his coffee. He straightened up and set the mug on the wooden tray table. "Thanks," he said to Mac. He gave me a half smile. "Take care of yourself, Sarah."

"Yeah, you too," I said.

Mac came over to me, put his arms around me and kissed the top of my head. "Let's go home," he said.

I started to say we could stay and realized I really didn't want to. "Sounds good," I said instead.

Mac rinsed out the mugs and the coffee maker and locked up. We headed out. "Can we go to your place?" I asked after a couple of minutes. Mac had a small apartment on the top floor of the shop.

"Sure," he said. He shot me a quick, sideways glance. He didn't ask why and I knew he wouldn't, still I wanted him to know what I was thinking.

"Everyone is probably still at Rose's. I don't want to have to explain why we're home early."

"That's what I figured," he said.

When we got to Mac's apartment he made grilled cheese sandwiches and we watched the original version of *The Day the Earth Stood Still*. It was one of my favorite old movies. "This 1951 version is the quintessential version," I told Mac. "No disrespect to Keanu Reeves, of course."

"Of course," he said.

When the movie ended I decided to head home.

"You can stay," Mac said. "Why don't you?"

I leaned over and kissed his cheek. "It's a very tempting offer but I need clean clothes and socks that fit better than the pair of yours I'm wearing. And I need to wash my hair and you don't have the right conditioner."

"Okay," he said, "but call me if you need me."

I promised I would. Then I had to kiss him again, which meant it took me longer to get going than I'd intended.

*   *   *

In the morning I came out of my apartment to find Elvis waiting patiently for me. "How was your night?" I asked.

He gave an enthusiastic meow and licked his whiskers. I wondered how many treats he'd had.

Rose stepped into the hallway then. "Good morning," she said. She smiled and handed me a small, blue and white casserole dish. "Chicken pot·pie. I saved you one. It should go in the refrigerator."

"Thank you," I said. I unlocked my door and took the food inside. I came back out, locked the door again and we headed out to my SUV. It was a gray, dull morning although the forecast was calling for sunshine later.

We headed for Second Chance, Elvis on the front seat next to Rose, and I realized both Rose and the cat were looking expectantly at me.

"You know," I said, watching them both out of the corner of my eye. "The question is how do you know?"

"In short, Ann, Clayton, Charlotte." Rose ticked off the names on the fingers of her left hand.

Ann was a librarian with excellent research skills. Like Rose she knew everyone in town. She lived close to Memphis. So did Clayton, who was Glenn McNamara's uncle and was also "seeing" Charlotte.

Charlotte Elliot and Rose had been friends as long as Rose and my grandmother had known each other. She was a retired principal whose former students were quick to wrap her in a hug and tell her how much she affected their lives if they met on the street. Charlotte's son, Nick, was one of my oldest friends and Rose had tried very hard to get the two of us together romantically. Nick's selling points had included the fact that he had great hair—which he did—and didn't snore, while my best feature had been my good teeth.

"I expected at least another couple of people involved somehow," I said.

"I'm striving for efficiency," Rose said. Then she put a hand on my arm. "Are you okay?"

That was Rose. She genuinely cared about other people's well-being.

"I am," I said. Elvis suddenly meowed loudly. "Yes, I see the man walking the dog." I gestured for the two of them to cross the street and the man raised a hand in thanks. Elvis was a bit of a backseat driver, one of his many quirks I'd learned about when he came to live with me.

I turned left and headed up the hill. "It was unsettling and sad to see the dead man," I said to Rose, "but I'm all right. It's not the first dead body I've seen."

"And what about Cleveland?" she said.

I hesitated for a moment. It didn't feel right to say that Cleveland had seemed very unsettled. "He's okay, given that he was the one who found the body," I said.

Rose shook her head. "You were a terrible liar when you were five, sweet girl, and you haven't gotten any better." She reached over to pat my arm. "Not that it's a bad thing."

I sighed. "I'm not lying exactly. It's just that I think finding the body was hard for Cleveland and I . . . I don't know how to help him. I don't want to push."

"First of all, perfectly understandable for Cleveland to feel unsettled. He found someone's body. How can you be okay after that? As for helping, just be his friend."

I stopped at a stop sign. Rose turned in her seat to look directly at me. "Are you all right, really?" she asked.

I blew out a breath. "I feel sad. I couldn't even see the man's face. There was a piece of tarp caught around his head, but nonetheless I feel bad that he's dead. Whatever life he had, whatever dreams and plans, it's all over now."

"'If there's another world, he lives in bliss; if there is none, he made the best of this,'" Rose said softly, and somehow Robert Burns's words made me feel a little better.

Chapter 3

When we arrived at Second Chance, Charlotte was already there. Mac had coffee for me that I gratefully accepted and Charlotte told Rose she'd made the tea.

"Thank you," Rose said. She headed upstairs to the staff room. For once Elvis didn't follow her. Instead he climbed onto a striped wood and canvas beach chair and began to wash his face.

"I have to go look for paint," Mac said. "I'll be in the workroom if you need me."

"You're probably already tired of the question, but are you all right?" Charlotte asked. I could see the concern in her dark eyes.

"I feel bad for the dead man and his family," I said, "but I'm fine. Have you heard anything?"

She shook her head and pushed her glasses up her nose. Even in flats she was an inch or so taller than me and she had lovely posture. "Not a thing. Do you have any idea who the man was?"

It was my turn to shake my head. "There was a

piece of old plastic tarp that had gotten wrapped around his head. I couldn't see his face."

"There are a lot more tourists in town these days," Charlotte said. "He could have been one."

"Michelle will probably be by sometime this morning to ask me more questions," I said. "Maybe she'll know something."

Half an hour later I was out in the workshop looking at two mid-century modern dining room chairs while Charlotte started packing the online orders that had come in overnight and watched the shop. I had a thing for chairs and these two were a find, made of cherrywood with elegant curved hoof legs. The fabric-covered seats were stained and I debated whether to try to clean the fabric or just re-cover the seats.

"What do you think?" I said to Elvis. He'd followed me out to the old garage, climbing on top of a tall dresser that had been sanded but not painted. "Clean or cover?"

He wrinkled his whiskers, then meowed loudly.

"Cover it is," I said. "Good choice. Let's go see what we have for fabric."

He jumped down from his perch and started across the parking lot. I followed. Inside the workroom Elvis launched himself onto the workbench and looked expectantly at me.

"Give me a minute," I said. I got a box of fabric from the shelves along the back wall and set it next to him. He immediately put a paw on top. "Oh, let me get that for you, your majesty," I said.

He flicked his tail at me. A lot of the time I had the

feeling Elvis understood sarcasm. I opened the top and started going through the material inside. Elvis poked his head inside the carton.

"This would go a lot easier if you'd move your giant head," I told him. The only response I got was a muffled murp from inside the box.

Eventually we settled on a length of silver-gray fabric with a faint sheen. I headed back outside and Elvis began washing his face. It seemed he felt his part of the job was done. I was halfway across the parking lot when Cleveland's truck pulled in. He got out and I walked over to him.

"Hey, Sarah," he said. "I just came by to make sure you were okay." He rolled his eyes. "Are you as sick of hearing that as I am?"

I nodded. "Oh yeah. I've been out here less than half an hour and in that time Mac brought me coffee and Charlotte brought me a cookie. Elvis even came to check on me."

"Memphis showed up with coffee this morning and not the crap from the convenience store."

"Everybody means well," I said.

"I know that wasn't your first dead body."

"I'm guessing it wasn't your first, either."

He shook his head. "No, it wasn't." He looked away for a moment, then his gaze came back to me. "Anytime you want to talk, I'm around."

I tucked a strand of hair that had slipped from my ponytail behind my ear. "That works both ways," I said.

Cleveland gestured at the back of his truck. "Since I'm here, you wanna take a look? I have a couple of boxes of Depression glass and an old chest I think you could probably do something with."

"Absolutely," I said.

He dropped the tailgate and climbed up into the truck bed while I leaned over the side. I ended up buying the wooden chest, an old quilt that I felt confident my friend Jess could restore and some of the Depression glass. After we'd put everything in the old garage I went over what was on my wish list—a couple of kitchen stools, a kid-size wooden table and chairs set, and any vintage galvanized washtubs he happened to come across.

"Washtubs?" Cleveland said, a frown creasing his forehead. "Really?"

"The last two I got from you sold half an hour after I put them in the shop," I said. "People use them for herb gardens, not for laundry, by the way."

"Well, good thing they do, or you and I would both be out of business."

Michelle pulled into the parking lot then.

"Figured we'd be doing this sometime," Cleveland said, inclining his head in her direction.

Michelle got out of her car and walked over to us. "Good morning," she said. She was wearing jeans and a jacket the color of toffee. "I'm glad you're here," she said to Cleveland. "I have a few more questions for both of you. This saves me a trip."

"Fine with me," Cleveland said. He glanced at me.

"Me too," I said.

"Cleveland, how did you come to see the body in the first place?" Michelle asked.

He swiped a hand across his chin. "When Memphis bought the property there was a lot of junk down along the water—bottles, cans, an old metal steamer trunk."

"The green one," I said.

He nodded.

"I sold it to a tourist from Maryland," I told Michelle.

"That doesn't surprise me," she said with a smile. Her attention went back to Cleveland.

"I got into the habit of checking to see if anything has washed up whenever I stop in at the house," he said.

"So you saw the body."

"I didn't know I was looking at a body. I just saw something large, tangled in seaweed and part of a tarp and floating not too far from shore. I went down to see what it was. It wasn't until I got close that I realized it was a . . . person. I could see they were dead. I called nine-one-one and I was trying to decide whether to leave the body where it was or pull it in onto the sand when Sarah showed up."

Michelle nodded and turned her attention to me. "So you saw Cleveland and what?"

"Mac and Memphis were in the garage talking. Memphis had told me where Cleveland was. I pretty much always have a list of things I'm looking for. I thought I'd ask him to keep an eye out. I could see there was something in the water but I didn't know what. I didn't realize it was a body until I got a lot closer." I rubbed my shoulder with one hand. "Cleveland said the person was dead and he had called nine-one-one. I could see he was right. I noticed the . . . body seemed to be getting pulled out into deeper water and I figured getting it onto shore was the lesser of two evils."

Cleveland nodded. "I thought she was right."

"It's fine," Michelle said. "Did you notice anything when you moved the body?"

"There was some kind of injury to the back of his head," Cleveland said. He looked at me, seemingly for confirmation.

"I saw that, too," I said. I lifted a hand to my head. "The left side."

Cleveland nodded again.

"Did either of you see anything else—anything that might have belonged to the dead man, any footprints, anything?"

I started to say no but then I remembered the backpack. "I saw a backpack," I said slowly.

I saw the memory flash in Cleveland's eyes. "I saw that, too," he said, gesturing with one hand. "It was a dark purplish-red color."

"Anything else?" Michelle asked.

"No," Cleveland said.

"No," I echoed.

"If either of you think of anything, no matter how inconsequential it may seem, please call me."

We both said we would.

"If that's it, I need to get going," Cleveland said.

"We're done. Thank you both," Michelle said.

He looked at me. "I'll keep an eye out for the things you're looking for."

"Thanks," I said.

"If you need anything . . ." He hesitated for a fraction of a second. "Yell."

"You too," I said.

Cleveland got into his truck and left. I turned to Michelle. "Has the dead man been identified yet?" I asked.

"He has," she said, "but we aren't releasing the name until all his family has been notified."

"He wasn't a tourist, was he?"

Her expression turned guarded. "Why do you say that?"

"Because I don't see how a tourist could have ended up out there. Memphis's property is not exactly close to anywhere a tourist would stay or spend time."

"No, he wasn't a tourist and that's all I can say." She smiled. "But you can share that with Rose once I'm gone."

I laughed. "Rose went to the dentist but I'll update her as soon as she gets back. And now I'm changing the subject. How about we have supper sometime soon?"

"I'd like that." She put a hand on the front of her jacket. Her phone was probably in an inside pocket. "I really have to get going," she said. We hugged and she got into her car.

I picked up the box with the pale green Depression glass soup bowls and headed for the shop. I'd get Avery to wash the bowls when she came in at lunchtime. Depression glass seemed to be very popular lately with tourists and I was expecting a couple of bus tours at the end of the week.

Mr. P. was in his office working at his computer. Not only did he have his private investigator's license, but he and Rose and Charlotte ran an investigative firm, Charlotte's Angels—the Angels, for short—out of my old sun porch. Like everything else he did, he was very good at the job. So was Rose. According to both of them, their age was an advantage. As Rose liked to say, "No one pays any attention to old people." Turned out that was very useful for finding out things people don't want you to know. I'd learned that people did tend to underestimate and dismiss Rose and her co-horts, but it rarely happened twice.

Mr. P. caught sight of me and waved me into the office. "Cleveland was here," he said.

I nodded.

He looks at the contents of the box and smiled. "Very nice. My mother had a set of bowls just like those." He nudged his glasses up his nose. "I saw Michelle," he said.

I set the box on the table he used for a desk. "She had a few more questions."

"Did she say anything about the deceased?"

I shook my head. "Just that he wasn't a tourist. She wouldn't tell me who he was because there are next of kin still to be notified."

I noticed the gleam in his eyes. I pointed a finger at him. "Alfred Peterson, you know the man's name, don't you?"

"I do," he said. He tapped the touchpad of his laptop and a photo of a man filled the screen. "His name is Michael Norris. Do you remember Rosie selling a dining room table to a man who didn't want the chairs?"

I smiled. "I do because I loved those chairs. They had tapered legs and a spindle back that were both painted black, with a stained seat."

He smiled back at me. "My dear, you have an affinity for every chair that passes through the shop and there's nothing wrong with that."

I studied the face on the computer screen. "I remember him."

Mr. P. nodded. "He bought the table and a set of all-white dishes, if I recall correctly."

I thought back to the day. It was over a year ago. Michael Norris and I had recognized each other from the Thursday Night Jam down at The Black Bear pub. He was tall with dark hair and a scar above his right eye. I could see the scar in the photo now, a faint white line etched on his face. "He thanked me for letting him buy just the table," I said. It was hard to put my memory of that man with the body I'd seen last night.

Rose came in then. "No cavities," she said with a smile. She glanced in the box. "Cleveland was here."

"He was," I said. "I bought another quilt, too."

"How is he?" Rose asked.

"He's good."

"Would you like me to take a look at that quilt?" Rose had an eye for fine details like missing stitches or worn areas of fabric.

"Please," I said. "And Avery can wash these bowls when she gets here." I rested one hand on the top of the box. "Michelle stopped by, too. All she'd say was that the dead man wasn't a tourist. And she told me I could tell you that."

Rose immediately looked at Mr. P.

He smiled at her. "His name was Michael Norris." He gestured at his laptop.

"He bought the table and the set of white dishes from that huge yard sale we went to in Rockport," Rose said. "That was more than a year ago."

I nodded.

Two frown lines formed between her eyebrows. "I wonder why he died," she said.

I shrugged. "It's probably too soon to tell. I'm guessing they'll do the autopsy today or tomorrow, but it's likely the man drowned." I remembered the wound on Norris's head. "It's possible he slipped on the rocks and hit his head."

Rose gave her head an impatient shake. "I said I wondered *why* he died, not *how.*"

And the conversation went off the road into the ditch. That happened with Rose.

"I don't know what you mean," I said.

"Why did someone kill Mr. Norris?" she said in that tone that told me she was trying hard to be patient, but what she was asking should be obvious.

"What on earth makes you think Michael Norris was murdered?" I said. Looking at Mr. P., even he seemed surprised by her allegation.

"What Michelle said, of course."

"All Michelle said was it was okay to tell you the dead man was not a tourist."

"Exactly," Rose said, smiling like I was her star pupil. "And *why* would that matter to me unless there was a possible future case for the Angels? And *how* would that happen unless Mr. Norris had been murdered?"

She reached over and patted my arm. "Do your best to keep up, sweetie." Then she took the box of Depression glass and left.

I stared after her. Rose could make gigantic leaps of logic sometimes. Sometimes they were right. I was acutely aware that Michelle had not said anything about Michael Norris having been murdered. But she hadn't said he hadn't been, either.

Chapter 4

I turned back to Mr. P. "What do you know about Michael Norris?" I asked. I knew he'd have some information.

"Not a lot, really," he said. "Mr. Norris owns—owned, I should say—a couple of rental properties here in town. He seems to have been a solitary person who mostly kept to himself."

That fit with the serious man I remembered.

"He has one younger sister, Joanna, who is a nurse."

"Do you think it's possible he was murdered?" I said.

"You saw the body," Mr. P. said. "So you're in a better position to make that determination than I am."

I shot him a look. "You're hedging."

He smiled. "Ask yourself how often Rosie is wrong about this kind of thing." He picked up his teacup and left.

I rubbed the space between my eyes with the heel of my hand. I was getting a headache.

I went back outside to the workshop. The silver-gray fabric would work well with the chairs. I just needed to take the seats apart. I set the quilt aside to look at later and crouched down to look more closely at the wooden chest. It didn't smell musty at all inside and I was pleased by the good shape it was in. I got to my feet as Mac came out of the back door.

"Hi," I said. "Did you make up your mind on the paint?"

"I did," he said. "It took a while because I got side-tracked helping Charlotte get a bed set up in the shop."

"Which one? We had two in the workroom."

"The one you sprayed with the dark bronze finish."

I gave him a teasing grin. "Oh, you mean the one where you flirted with the woman in heels higher than Liz wears and got us twenty percent off."

Mac laughed. "I think she was more interested in Alfred than me."

"I saw her checking out your stern as you walked away."

That made him laugh even harder. "She was old enough to be my mother!"

I hooked a finger in the neck of his shirt and pulled him toward me. "I think the woman had good taste no matter which one of you she liked the look of." I glanced around and kissed him. I let him go and reached up and rubbed my forehead again.

"Got a headache?" Mac asked.

I nodded. "A bit of one."

"Michelle?"

"Not exactly," I said. "The dead man's name is

Michael Norris. I got his name from Mr. P., not Michelle. It turns out he bought a table from us more than a year ago. Didn't want the chairs."

Mac nodded slowly. "I remember him. It was a tight fit to get that table into his SUV. I always wondered how he got it out without help. Did he have any family? A spouse? Kids?"

I shook my head. "Just a sister, according to Alfred." I hesitated. "Rose thinks he was murdered."

Mac frowned like he hadn't heard me properly. "Murdered? Why?"

"Apparently because Michelle told me that I could tell Rose the dead man wasn't a tourist. Rose felt it was a clue that Mr. Norris's death hadn't been accidental. Don't ask me to explain the logic because I can't follow it."

"That's a bit of a leap even for Rose."

"Did you pick her up after her dentist appointment?" I asked. I had a niggling feeling Rose was already investigating, even though we had no client and there probably was no murder.

"I didn't," he said. "I told her to call me when she was done but someone dropped her off. She said she met somebody she knew."

I picked up my empty coffee cup. "She's up to something," I said. "I'll be right back."

Rose was standing in the middle of the Angels' office wearing one of the long aprons she usually wore in the store.

"Rose Jackson, what did you do?" I said.

"I went to the dentist," she said. "I told you I had no cavities." Nice teeth were important to Rose.

I set my mug on the edge of Mr. P.'s desk. "You're a much better liar than I am, but I don't buy your so-called reason for thinking Michael Norris was murdered."

"Just tell her," Mr. P. said.

I folded my arms. "Yes, tell me."

Rose's chin came up and she straightened her shoulders. "Fine. But I want it on the record that I didn't go looking for this information. It just fell in my lap."

"Duly noted," I said.

"I knew Michael Norris was the man whose body you found before I left for the dentist."

"How?" I said.

"I have connections," she said. "That's really all you need to know. Anyway, I remembered talking to him while I wrapped the dishes. I'd asked where he lived." She glanced at Mr. P. "You remember Merton, Alfred's friend?"

"I remember," I said. Merton had a seagull—Mr. P. insisted the birds were very smart—that had "helped" in one of the Angels' previous cases. In fact it was possible that Tippi—yes, the bird was named after actress Tippi Hedren—might someday ask us to do a favor for it.

"It turns out that Mr. Norris lived very close to Merton. I was sitting in the dentist's waiting room wondering if perhaps I should talk to Merton about his neighbor when he walked in." She held out both hands. "If that wasn't a sign from the universe that I should, then what would be?"

"And?" I said.

Rose frowned. "And what? I talked to him for a good five minutes until his hygienist called him. They were a little backed up."

"And what did Merton tell you?" I realized I had overenunciated the words.

"He said that Michael Norris was very quiet and kept to himself. His parents had died several years ago and his sister was his only family. They were very close. And he said Michael was a little apprehensive about Tippi." She gave me a triumphant look. "And that's when I knew he had been murdered—Michael, obviously, not Merton."

I rubbed my forehead again. The headache wasn't getting any better.

"You figured out that Michael Norris was murdered because he didn't like seagulls?" I said. That made less sense than the earlier explanation.

Rose frowned. "Well, now that just sounds silly. I figured it out because Michael didn't like the water. He couldn't swim very well."

"Are you sure?" I said.

"I don't see why Merton would lie about something like that."

"Michael Norris didn't like the water," I repeated slowly.

"So what was he doing down there *by the water*?" Rose asked. "He didn't live anywhere close to Memphis. It doesn't make sense."

It didn't make sense, I thought. "Maybe there's a logical explanation."

"Maybe there is, and if you have one I would love to hear it."

"I don't," I said. I held up a hand. "At least not right now."

"Well, you know where I stand," she said.

"So what are you going to do?" I asked.

"I'm not going to do anything. Michelle is very good at her job, and if she hasn't come to the same conclusion, she will soon. And we don't have a client, so we don't have a case."

"Okay, then," I said. I picked up my mug and went upstairs for another cup of coffee. When I came back down Charlotte was showing a customer a wooden serving cart. It was a piece I'd bought from Cleveland.

I went back outside.

Mac was looking at the hinges on the wooden chest. "So?" he said.

I exhaled loudly and took a drink from my mug before answering. "So Rose talked to Merton—he was at the dentist as well—and according to him and maybe Tippi for all I know, Michael Norris couldn't swim very well and didn't like the water."

"So how did he end up *in* the water?"

"According to Rose because he was murdered."

"Do you think she could be right?"

"I don't know." I flashed to the injury on the back of Michael Norris's head. "And even if she is, it doesn't mean we'll end up involved. Rose said we have no client so the Angels have no case and I'm going to take her at her word."

Mac smiled. "Are you sure you should?"

I laughed. "No. I know firsthand how Rose can be when she gets her mind set on something, but for now I'm trying not to make myself crazy. As Rose pointed out, Michelle is good at what she does and she'll figure out what happened."

I didn't want to talk about Michael Norris's death anymore. I didn't want to think about it. "I'm going to Glenn's," I said abruptly. "I forgot lunch."

Glenn McNamara's sandwich shop and bakery was one of my favorite places in town.

"Go," Mac said. "I'll hold down the fort."

I went back inside and got my wallet, stuffing it in the pocket of my jeans. Then I drove to the sandwich shop. It was early so it was very quiet, with just a couple of customers at tables. Glenn was wiping the counter when I walked in. He was tall with the build of a former college football player—which he was. "Hey, Sarah," he said. "I was hoping you'd be in." He wasn't smiling.

"Is everything all right?" I said. The air suddenly felt heavy, the way it did before a thunderstorm.

"Can we talk for a minute?"

I nodded. "Sure."

Glenn stuck his head into the kitchen and called for Sophia. "Could you look after things out here for a few minutes?" he asked. "I want to talk to Sarah."

Sophia was a student who worked part-time at the shop. She'd created a gingerbread cupcake that Glenn had added to the menu. "Of course," she said. She smiled and gave me a little wave. She was barely five feet tall with brown skin, dark eyes and gorgeous braids, which she wore tied back under a ball cap when she was working.

Glenn led me over to a table in the corner and we both sat down. "What's going on?" I said.

He swiped a hand across his chin. "Rumor has it you were there last evening when Cleveland found Michael Norris's body."

"I was." It seemed everyone knew it was Michael Norris who had died, whether Michelle wanted that information out or not.

Glenn stared down at the table. After a moment he looked up at me once again. "Do you know what happened? I know you and Michelle Andrews are friends. Did she . . . did she tell you anything?"

I shook my head. "I don't know anything more than you do. All I can tell you is Cleveland found the body and I helped him get it to shore. Michelle hasn't told me anything. That's not how it works."

"I know, but I was hoping . . ." He didn't finish the sentence. He seemed to be working something out and I waited without saying anything, giving him time to fix on whatever it was that he needed to settle in his head. Finally he cleared his throat and said, "I've been friends with Michael Norris since eighth grade, although we hadn't spent much time together recently."

"Oh, Glenn, I'm sorry," I said.

He almost smiled. "Thanks. There were four of us, Michael, me, Andrew Lewis and Freddie—short for Frederica—Black. We called ourselves the Four Musketeers. Not very creative."

"I like it," I said.

"Michael was a year younger than the rest of us because he skipped a grade in school. I can promise you that he never would have been on that stretch of beach willingly. Never. Neither would I." He said the words with complete certainty.

"I don't understand," I said. "What is it about that particular place?"

He sighed. "Almost fifteen years ago I had a Fourth of July party on the beach behind my uncle Clayton's house. He was away and I was house-sitting. Andrew, Freddie and Michael were there and a few other friends. We were all in our early twenties. Some people were in grad school. Some of us were still trying to figure out what we wanted to do with our lives." He gave me a wry smile. "The party kind of spread out down as far as what's Memphis Guitard's property now. We often hung out down there because the house was empty at the time. Freddie . . . Freddie drowned after being pushed off a breakwater."

I pulled one hand into a fist and pressed it against my mouth.

"Andrew had been seen arguing with Freddie by several people right before she was believed to have gone in the water. They were out on the rocks. He was charged with manslaughter in her death and he went to prison."

I felt as though my insides had tied themselves into a knot.

"I go to Clayton's place all the time but I haven't been down by that breakwater since that night. And I don't intend to go down there. Ever." Glenn shook his head. "There's no way Michael would have been there, either. He wasn't that crazy about the beach anyway because he could barely swim. The night Freddie died was the worst night of my life and of Michael's, too. He wouldn't go anywhere near that stretch of beach."

I struggled to find the right words. "You said it was almost fifteen years ago. Maybe it was some kind of emotional pilgrimage."

Glenn shook his head. "Michael wasn't that kind of person. You're just going to have to take my word on that."

I nodded. "Okay. So how can I help?"

"I need to talk to the police and I need them to take me seriously."

"Michelle will," I said. "She's not a judgmental person and she'll listen to what you have to say."

Glenn looked down at the table again and then looked at me. "Even if I tell her I think Michael was murdered?"

Chapter 5

I didn't know what to say.

Glenn held out both hands. "Yeah, I know how far-fetched it sounds, but it's the only explanation I have for what happened that makes any sense to me."

"Okay," I said. "Then tell that to Michelle. I promise she's not going to dismiss what you tell her without checking everything out."

"I'm not the only person who knows how Michael felt about the water," he said. "That won't be hard to confirm."

I thought about what Rose had learned from Merton. Michael Norris's dislike of water seemed to be common knowledge. "You said your friend died almost fifteen years ago, so Michelle would have access to those case files," I said. "And they'll be doing an autopsy, probably sometime today or tomorrow. Michelle should have a better idea of what's going on pretty quickly. If you think it would help, I can call Nick."

Nick Elliot wasn't just Charlotte's son, he was also an investigator for the medical examiner's office.

"That's okay, I can call Nick. I didn't think of that."

"Nick's known you a long time and he'll take whatever you tell him seriously."

Glenn nodded. "It changed everything," he said, "Freddie's death, I mean. Maybe if I had—"

I didn't let him finish. "Don't fall into that trap, Glenn. 'That way madness lies.'"

He smiled. "King Lear."

I smiled back at him. "Well, when you hang around former teachers you pick up some things."

"Thanks for listening," he said.

"Hey, anytime," I said. "Talk to Michelle. Talk to Nick. They'll listen to you."

"I will." He got to his feet. "Did you come in for lunch before I hijacked you?"

I stood up as well. "You can hijack me anytime, and yes, I am looking for lunch."

I ordered a roast beef and cheddar sandwich on one of Glenn's whole-grain cheese rolls along with a date square. Sophia started on my sandwich. Glenn got the date square. "How's the boat coming?" he asked as he tucked it in a small, waxed paper bag.

"Mac's making really good progress," I said. "I know a lot about repurposing things but there's no way I could tackle a project like that."

"Neither could I," Glenn said. "I just tried to put together a nightstand I bought at one of those big box stores. It was a flat box full of pieces and no written instructions, just pictures of little stick men."

I frowned. "Wait a minute, I just sold you a night-stand."

Glenn grinned and said, "Exactly."

I realized what he meant and laughed.

He handed me the sandwich and date square. "It's on the house."

"No, you can't do that," I said.

"Yeah I can," he said. "I own the place."

"Thank you," I said. "Will you be at the jam to-night?"

He nodded. "Wouldn't miss it."

The Thursday Night Jam happened pretty much every Thursday night at The Black Bear pub. The house band—owner Sam Newman and his buddies—played classic rock and roll and anyone was welcome to sit in for a song or two, or the whole night.

"If there's anything I can do to help, please ask," I said.

He nodded. "I will. Thanks."

I drove back to the shop thinking Rose might turn out to be right, and hoping somehow that she didn't.

It was a busy afternoon. We had an unexpected tour bus stop in and the Depression glass soup bowls sold, along with the two wood and canvas beach chairs, several vases, a music box and a very ornate set of gold and silver dishes that Rose carefully packed with recycled tissue paper and bubble wrap. At the end of the day Rose drove home with Elvis and me. Mac and Mr. P. left together because they were going to play poker with some of Mr. P.'s friends and were going out for supper first.

"Will Nick be at the jam?" Rose asked.

"As far as I know," I said. "I haven't heard differently."

I waited for Rose to say something else, but she didn't. After a couple of minutes of silence I glanced over at her, sitting in the passenger seat, hands folded in her lap.

"Aren't you going to ask me to ask Nick if he's heard anything?" I said.

Rose smiled. "I was hoping you would offer without me having to ask."

I laughed. "You don't even know if this is Nick's case. Neither do I. I left before anyone from the medical examiner's office arrived."

"Even if it's not his case, it doesn't mean he hasn't heard anything," Rose said. "And he might be in the mood for sharing."

"No promises," I said, "but I can ask."

Rose reached over and patted my arm. "Well, if it will make you feel better, go ahead."

Out of the corner of my eye I could see her smile.

When we got to the house Rose gave me a hug and told me to have fun. I opened our apartment door and Elvis immediately climbed to the top of his cat tower—which Mr. P. had made for him—and flopped on his stomach with his paws hanging down.

I scratched the top of his head. "You're so dramatic. Five minutes and I'll get your supper."

I washed my face, put on a little makeup, pulled my hair back in a loose knot and changed into jeans, a red-and-black-striped long-sleeved T-shirt and my favorite low black boots. I grabbed a hoodie and my bag and went to give Elvis his supper and fresh water.

He lifted his head to watch me but didn't come down until I was done. He eyed the food and then looked at me and meowed.

"You're welcome," I said. "I won't be late and the TV is on the timer." Elvis was still a devoted *Jeopardy!* fan, even after the death of Alex Trebek.

I was the first to arrive at the pub. Usually Jess got there first. She was probably still working on something in her shop. Jess was an incredible seamstress and she co-owned a little shop nearby.

Sam was standing by the bar and he smiled when he caught sight of me. Sam Newman was my late dad's best friend and the two of us had always had a close connection. I gave him a hug. "I hope you're in good voice tonight," I said.

He laughed. "Nope. I just have my usual voice."

I nudged him with my shoulder. "You're such a smartass."

"Leo Kingston is in town and he's going to be sitting in tonight," Sam said.

"Leo Kingston?" I frowned. "Hang on, didn't he used to play with you and Dad?"

Sam nodded. "Back in the day. Leo's a great guitar player and he's been making a living as a studio musician for years." He raised one eyebrow. "I'm going to have to up my game tonight."

"Your game is always top-notch," I said.

Sam smiled, then his expression turned serious. "I heard about you and Cleveland finding Michael Norris's body yesterday. I was really sorry to hear he was dead."

"You knew him." I wasn't really surprised. Sam knew all the regulars at the jam.

He nodded. "Yeah, I did. I gave Michael guitar lessons, must be close to twenty years ago now. And he was here almost every Thursday night."

"I remembered seeing him."

Sam pointed to the far corner of the room. "Always sat over there. Swore that part of the room had the best acoustics." He smiled. "Michael was a pretty decent guitar player, you know. More than once I tried to get him to sit in for a couple of songs but he always said no."

Sam glanced around the room. The place was beginning to fill up. He focused on me again. "I'm guessing you probably heard about what happened fifteen years ago out there where you and Cleveland found Michael's body."

"You mean about the girl getting pushed off the rocks and drowning?" I said.

"Yeah." He shrugged. "That whole thing changed Michael. He pulled into himself and he pulled away from people. I can't make sense out of what he was doing out there, of all places. You know, he told me once that that was one piece of ground he was never going to set foot on again."

One of the servers came out of the kitchen then and told Sam he was needed back there.

He shook his head. "You know what they say, no rest for the wicked."

"Go save the day," I said.

He smiled. "I'm glad you're here."

"Nowhere else I'd be on a Thursday night." I gave him another quick hug. "Love you."

"Back at you, kiddo," he said.

I turned and saw Jess coming in the door. I waved. She smiled and pointed to a table across the room. We grabbed it just in time. It was going to be a full house. It pretty much always was, even on the coldest Thursday nights in January and February.

"Sorry I'm late," Jess said as she pulled off her sweater. It was a deep plum color, flattering to her dark hair and fair skin.

"I just got here myself," I said. "I was talking to Sam."

"Is Nick coming?"

"Far as I know."

Jess pointed to the chair next to me. "Okay, then don't let anyone swipe that chair. Have you had supper?"

I shook my head.

"Me neither." She flipped her hair back over her shoulder. "Want me to grab a waiter?"

"Yes," I said, "because we both know if I try to catch the attention of one it will be forever before we get anything to eat."

Jess had some kind of uncanny way to snag the attention of waiters and store clerks. I watched her look around the room, somehow catch a waiter's eye and smile. The young man immediately started in our direction.

I shook my head, amazed at how that always worked.

"You know, I could stand on top of this table and do semaphore with my hoodie and I still wouldn't be able to get a waiter's attention."

Jess just grinned. "It's my superpower," she said.

She ordered a BLT when the waiter got to the table.

"That sounds good," I said. "I'll have the same."

"Anything else?" the waiter asked.

"Wanna split an order of sweet potato fries?" I said.

Jess nodded. "Absolutely." She also ordered our usual chips and salsa.

Once the waiter was gone she pulled her chair a little closer to mine. "I heard about what happened last night. I'm really sorry. It must have been horrible for both of you."

"It was the last thing that I expected to happen," I said.

"I know Michael Norris's sister, Joanna. She shops at the store pretty regularly. Michael is . . . was her only family, as far as I know. Those two were tight."

I stared up at the ceiling for a moment. "I hate even thinking about how she must feel."

"I think we're guilty of forgetting that not everyone can swim and even when someone can, it doesn't mean they can't drown."

I nodded. Maybe Michael Norris had drowned. Maybe he had gone down to the stretch of beach because the anniversary of his friend's death was coming up soon. Until the medical examiner made a determination about cause of death, everything else was just speculation.

The food and Nick both arrived at the same time. He stepped over the back of the chair next to me and sat down, reaching for a chip at the same time. Sam and the guys were just coming out to the small stage.

"Good timing, big guy," Jess said.

Nick smiled. "The key to a happy life." He shot me a look and I wondered if he was almost late because he was working on something related to Michael Norris's death.

The guys were fantastic. I studied Leo Kingston, thinking that he looked familiar. I wasn't sure if I just wanted him to because of his tenuous connection to my father, or if he really did. He was very tall, easily six foot four, with a shaved head, a gray and brown beard and glasses.

"Do you know who the guy sitting in is?" Nick asked, leaning back in his chair as the guys took a brief break. "He's good."

"Yeah, he is," I said. "His name is Leo Kingston. He used to play with Sam." I paused for a moment. "And my dad."

Nick just nodded. I didn't talk about my dad a lot and he knew not to push.

Jess stood up. "I'll be right back. There's someone I need to talk to."

As soon as Jess was out of hearing range Nick turned to me. "Thanks for getting Glenn to call me. He told me he talked to you."

"You're welcome," I said. "I hope he gave you something useful."

He laughed. "You're getting better at fishing for information."

I propped one elbow on the table and leaned my head against my hand. "Well, I've spent a lot of time with Rose. You might say I've learned at the feet of the master."

His smile faded. "They're not involved in this, are they?"

"No," I said. I hadn't told Rose about my conversation with Glenn. I considered him a friend and I didn't want to violate his privacy. "Do you have a cause of death yet?"

He shook his head. "The autopsy is scheduled for tomorrow morning."

I hesitated, thinking maybe I should just stop talking and not tell Nick anything that I knew would frustrate him. On the other hand I didn't want to hold back any bit of information that might be helpful, especially if it turned out that Michael Norris *had* been murdered.

"Rose and her crew aren't exactly involved, but she did get some information from Mr. P.'s friend Merton," I said.

"The guy with the pigeon."

"Seagull. Tippi."

"Tippi," he repeated.

"After Tippi Hedren who starred in *The Birds*. Which really isn't important. Rose learned the same thing about Michael Norris not liking the water from Merton."

Nick laced his fingers together and rested his hands on the back of his head. "And he knew this how?" He didn't even try to hide his skepticism.

"One, because they were neighbors and, two, because Merton knows everything. He talks to everyone. He's like Rose in a bad toupée and of course with the seagull."

Nick eyed me, a look of suspicion on his face. "There's something you're not telling me, Sarah," he said.

"The Angels don't have a client and they don't have a case," I said, hoping that would satisfy him.

I should have known it wouldn't.

"There's a big but coming, isn't there?" he said.

I took a deep breath and let it out. "Rose thinks Michael Norris was murdered," I said.

Chapter 6

Nick swore and made a face. "You just said Rose and the rest of them weren't involved." He gave me an accusatory look.

"They're not," I said, sitting upright again. "I told you. There's no client. There's no investigation." I held up a hand to stop whatever objection he was about to make. "And to be fair it's not like Rose went looking to get involved in this. She heard what happened, and then she went to the dentist and by chance met Merton in the waiting room. They started talking. Merton and Michael Norris were neighbors, so of course he and Rose talked about Norris's death. Merton told her that Michael didn't like the water. You know how Rose's mind works."

"I know exactly how Rose's mind works, how all of their minds work," he said.

I didn't like his tone. "Hey, don't be so condescending," I said, glaring at him. "They've solved more than one crime because of the way they think."

"I'm sorry," he said. He stretched his arms up over his head for a moment. "Since you talked to Glenn you know that both he and Norris have a connection to a death that happened out at the same spot close to fifteen years ago."

I nodded. "Glenn told me."

"Look, Sarah, this isn't a case I want to see Rose and Alfred and my mother mixed up in."

"Is there any case you want to see them mixed up in?"

He held out both hands in a gesture of surrender. "Fine, you got me. No. You know there isn't."

"Nick, relax," I said. "I don't see how they're going to get pulled into this one." Even as I said the words I felt a tightness in my chest that told me I might have just said something I was going to regret.

Nick reached over and swiped the last two cold sweet potato fries.

"Hey, what was in the backpack?" I said.

"What backpack?" It was only because I'd known Nick all my life that I knew by the way he casually leaned back in his chair, seemingly unconcerned by the question, that he was in fact trying to avoid answering it.

"The backpack that was on the beach by the rocks. It belonged to Michael Norris, didn't it?"

"C'mon, don't ask me questions like that," he said.

"Why?" I said. "Odds are it was his, so why not just admit it. He was on the beach. The backpack was on the beach. It's kind of obvious."

"It's not the kind of information I can give you."

For some reason I was annoyed and frustrated by his response. "Why not?" I snapped.

"Because you don't have any right to that information. You have no connection to the case whatsoever."

I didn't like his words or his tone. I leaned closer to him. "Really?" I said, my voice edged with anger. "I helped Cleveland drag Michael Norris's dead body out of the water so it wouldn't float away, so don't say I have no connection to the case. He was dead. Tangled in seaweed and an old tarp *and dead.*"

Nick had the good grace to look a little chagrined.

"I'd much rather not be connected to all of this," I said, in a softer voice, "but I am. *I am.*"

I closed my eyes for a moment and took a couple of slow, deep breaths. When I opened them again Nick said, "Picnic stuff."

I looked at him, and frowned. "Picnic stuff?"

He nodded. "That's what was in the backpack. And yes, it did belong to Norris."

Jess came back then with more chips and salsa, and people began to clap as the band returned. Jess leaned toward me as she snagged a chip. "Is everything okay?" she asked in a low voice.

I shot Nick a quick glance. "Everything's good," I said.

The second set was even better than the first and I found myself thinking of my father when Leo sang harmony with Sam. The feeling wasn't painful, just a little sad.

Afterward, I decided I wanted to meet Leo.

"I'm sorry I was a jerk," Nick said as I pulled on my hoodie.

Jess gave him a look. "I have no idea what you did," she said, "but yes, you probably were, and it wasn't the first time."

"I overreacted a bit," I said, "so one cancels the other out."

Nick looked at me. "Are we good?" he said.

I nodded. "We are."

He turned to Jess then. "I can drop you."

"Do you need me?" she asked, raising one eyebrow.

"I'm fine," I said. "I'm going to talk to Sam for a minute and then I'm going home."

Jess wrapped me in a hug. "If you need me, you call me," she whispered.

"I will," I said. Nick and Jess left and I walked over to the stage area.

Sam and Leo were surrounded by several people, but when Sam spotted me he seemed to realize why I had come over. He touched Leo on the arm and said something in his ear. Leo looked in my direction and the two of them started toward me. As they approached he smiled.

"Leo, this is Sarah," Sam said.

"Sarah Grayson. It must be at least twenty-five years since I last saw you. This is . . ." He shook his head. "This is unexpected and wonderful."

I smiled back at him. "You were so good."

"Thank you," he said. "I guess I wasn't as rusty as I was afraid I'd be. Tell me, how's your mother?"

"She's good," I said. "She writes a children's book

series and she remarried years ago. She and my step-dad live in New Hampshire."

"I'm so glad to hear that. Please give her my best next time you talk to her."

"I will," I said. "Are you staying in town? I'd love to hear you perform again."

"I'm trying to twist his arm," Sam said.

I smiled. "I hope it works."

"What about you, Sarah?" Leo asked. "Do you play or sing?"

"She does both," Sam said before I could answer. "But I haven't had much success convincing her to join us."

Leo raised an eyebrow. "I could probably be persuaded to sit in again if you'd join in for a couple of songs. I'm guessing you have a guitar."

I thought about my dad's guitar sitting in a closet back at the house. "I do, but I haven't played in a while."

"Doesn't seem like a hard audience to please," he said. "I don't mean to put pressure on you but the times I played with your father were some of the best times in my life and I'd love to play with his daughter."

All of a sudden there was a lump in my throat. I looked around. There were more people waiting to talk to both of them. "I should get going," I said.

Leo smiled. "I'm glad you came to say hello. I hope it's not another twenty-five years before I see you again."

"I'll walk you out," Sam said.

"I meant what I said," I told him as we headed for the door. "It was so good to see Leo perform. You never do that Eagles song and it made me happy to hear it."

"I was surprised how good it felt to sing it. Thinking about your father should make us feel that way. He'd hate it if it didn't. And for the record, he'd want you to play his guitar. Think about what Leo said."

I gave him a hug, said good night and left.

Friday was a very quiet day at the shop. I finished cleaning the chairs I'd been working on, got the seats off and got them re-covered. When I took them inside Charlotte and Avery decided those chairs would work better around a small, round wooden dining table that they had in the window display than the black chairs they had originally chosen almost two weeks ago. The table had X-shaped legs that I'd painted a dark, smoky gray. I had to admit I did like the look of the table and chairs with their newly covered seats. I carried the black ones out to the workroom and put them back with the others in my collection, wondering if I could find room for a couple of them in my apartment.

I found myself thinking about Michael Norris's autopsy from time to time during the day, wondering if it was over and whether or not the medical examiner had determined the cause of death.

That night Mac and I went out for supper to Avery's favorite vegan restaurant, Seasons. The restaurant was close enough to walk to from my apartment. It took up the main floor of a building that at one time had housed a sailmaker. They served delicious vegan food and the menu changed according to what was in season. I was getting to be as big a fan of the restaurant as Avery was. The atmosphere was very welcoming with wide-planked floors, strings of warm, white lights and pale green walls.

We chose a table by the window and on Avery's recommendation ordered risotto with leeks, spinach and butternut squash. It was as good as promised. We talked about Mac's brother, Jameis, who Mac hoped was coming for a visit at the end of the month. By the time we shared a slice of cake and headed for home I felt much better.

Saturday morning when I got to the shop there was a car in the lot. "Isn't that Maud Fitch?" I said to Elvis. Maud and her wife ran the Hearthstone Inn, a beautifully restored 1830s Victorian overlooking the water at Windspeare Point.

The cat put his two front paws on the dashboard and peered out the window, then he looked at me and meowed. It sounded like a yes to me.

I parked and Maud was already walking toward us as I got out of the SUV. Elvis jumped down after me.

"Sarah, I have a small problem," she said, skipping pleasantries altogether.

"How can I help?" I said.

"We have an afternoon tea planned today."

I smiled. "I know. I left it too late to get tickets."

"Help me out of this mess I'm in and I will deliver afternoon tea here to the shop," she said. She seemed a bit frazzled, which wasn't like Maud. She used to be an emergency room nurse.

"What happened?"

"In a word, Michelangelo."

Michelangelo was her cat. "I put a cloth on the sideboard. It had fringe and you can probably guess the rest *and* I need nineteen cups and saucers by one thirty this afternoon. Can you help?"

Avery was coming along the sidewalk. "I think so," I said, "but give me a second and I'll tell you for sure."

Avery started across the parking lot and I beckoned her over. "How many cups and saucers do we have in the shop?" I said. I knew she'd know the answer.

"Six in a set of dishes and nine more for planters," she said at once.

"That's fifteen. We need four more."

"What for?" Avery asked.

I explained about Michelangelo and the fringe.

"That's a cat for you," she said. "Did you ask Rose?"

I frowned. "Did I ask Rose for what?" I said.

"For cups and saucers. She'd lend you four."

I smiled. "She absolutely would." I looked at Maud. "Are you sure nineteen is enough?"

She nodded. "Could I take the fifteen you have now?"

"Sure, I'll pack them for you," Avery said before I could answer. The three of us headed for the back door. "How long is the sideboard?" Avery asked Maud.

"It's long," Maud said. "Sixty inches."

"We have a very pretty pale blue cloth that would just fit it, nothing hanging down on the sides," Avery said.

Maud smiled. "I'll take that, too."

In the end she left with the cups and saucers, the

cloth for the sideboard and two vases that Avery had filled with paper flower branches she'd made.

"Thank you for packing all the cups and saucers and for suggesting the cloth," I said. Avery had a way of putting things together that would never have occurred to me, and making them work.

She shrugged. "No problem," she said, but I caught a glimpse of a smile.

Two bus tours kept us busy all afternoon and I was happy to have spaghetti with Elvis and watch *Dateline* while Mac worked on the boat. He showed up with half an hour left in the program holding a plate with two pieces of chocolate cake.

"I brought cake," he said, holding out the plate with a flourish.

I eyed the plate. "That's my grandmother's chocolate cake with mocha frosting," I said. "You didn't make that."

Mac grinned. "I didn't say I made it. I said I brought it and I did, from the bottom of the stairs to your door." He leaned over and kissed my cheek. "That's from Isabel, too." I smiled and thought how lucky I was to have Gram and John in town more or less all the time now.

We sat on the sofa with the cake and I brought Mac up to date on *Dateline* during the commercials so we could watch the last part together.

Sunday morning Mac headed out early to help a friend do some work on his boat. I went for a long run and met Jess for brunch—blueberry pancakes and bacon—and a trip to a large flea market in Rockport.

Monday morning Mr. P. was waiting in the hall-way. "Good morning," he said. He was wearing the dark blue jacket Rose had convinced him to buy.

I studied him for a moment. "Rose is right," I said. "You do look good in that shade of blue."

"Thank you, my dear," he said. "I've learned Rosie is generally right about that kind of thing. By the way, she'll be right out. She decided at the last minute that she needed to replenish the tea bags."

I smiled. "It's okay. I'm a bit early."

Elvis padded down the hallway to wait outside Rose's door.

"Is there any chance she might be replenishing the cookies?" I asked Mr. P.

"I can neither confirm nor deny that," he said.

Rose stepped out of her apartment then. She smiled at Elvis. "Good morning," she said. "How nice of you to wait for me. Did you have a good weekend?"

He meowed loudly.

"Splendid," she said.

She turned and smiled at me. "Did you have a good weekend?" she asked.

"I did," I said. "Jess and I went to that big flea market in Rockport yesterday."

We headed outside.

I gestured at the SUV. "I bought a hall table with two loose legs, five teacups to replace the ones Maud bought, a vintage Sunbeam Mixmaster and a head-board and footboard for a twin bed."

"Oh, what color is the Mixmaster?" Rose asked.

I grinned. "Turquoise."

She clapped her hands together and grinned back at me. "I can think of two collectors who will want it."

"It's in excellent shape and even comes with the bowls."

We headed to Second Chance. I parked and Rose went to open the back door. Mr. P. helped me carry my finds into the workroom. Mac came out to look at the headboard and footboard. They were painted a vivid red-brown shade.

"What would you call this color?" he asked.

"Barbecue sauce," Mr. P. said.

I nodded. "Yes. But both pieces are all wood and the panels that make up the structure are solid."

"What are you thinking for color?" Mac said as he ran a hand over the footboard.

"Cranberry red," I said.

Mac looks surprised.

"People seem to be looking for color instead of just white and black." I showed him the waist-high hall console table. "It has one small drawer, which doesn't close smoothly, and something is off with two of the legs because it's a little wobbly. That's probably why I got it for such a steal."

"We'll put it in the workshop and I'll see what I can do. It has a definite cant to the left," Mac said.

"I have faith in you," I said.

Rose had her apron on when I went back into the shop. I showed her two boxes of books that needed to be packed to send to two different collectors. "I'm going up to check the online orders," I said.

I was halfway up the stairs when someone came in

the front door. I stopped and looked to see who it was. Rose looked up from the books she was stacking on the cash desk. It was Glenn.

"I'm glad you're both here," he said. "I need your help."

"What's wrong?" I asked. I had a feeling I knew the answer. I felt a shiver crawl up my spine. Rose would say a goose just walked over my grave.

Glenn swiped a hand over his chin. "I'm pretty sure the police think I killed Michael Norris."

Chapter 7

I came back down the stairs and Rose crossed the room to join me.

"What happened?" I asked Glenn.

He took a deep breath and exhaled slowly. "I talked to Nick a few days ago. I thought everything was good. Then this morning they asked me down to the police station to question me about Michael's death. I didn't kill him. You know that, don't you?"

"Of course we know that," I said.

Rose put a hand on my arm. "Alfred is in the office," she said. "Take Glenn back there and send Mac in."

"Good idea," I said.

I led Glenn back to the Angels' sun porch office, where Mr. P. was working on his computer. He looked up and smiled. "Hello, Glenn," he said. He gave me a questioning look.

"Glenn needs our help," I said. "I'm just going to get Mac, and Rose will be here in a minute."

Mr. P. nodded. "Come have a seat," he said to Glenn.

I put a hand on Glenn's arm. "I'll be right back and we'll figure this out."

I went out the back door and hurried across the empty lot, glad that it was early on a Monday and there were no customers.

Mac had the drawer from the console table up on a couple of sawhorses. "I need you to watch the shop," I said, a bit breathlessly. I had almost been running. "Glenn is here. The police questioned him a little while ago."

Mac frowned. "They can't seriously consider him a suspect."

"I don't know at this point," I said.

Mac closed and locked the door and we walked over to the shop. "Take as long as you need," he said. "I can handle any customers."

"I didn't mean to screw up your morning," Glenn said when I stepped back into the Angels' office. He rubbed his hands absently together.

"You didn't," I said.

Rose came with tea for herself and Mr. P. and coffee for Glenn and me. The Angels ran on tea and Rose believed it righted a lot of wrongs. She directed Glenn to sit at our long meeting table and set a tall mug in front of him. "Tell us what happened," she said.

"The police showed up at the shop early this morning and asked me to come down to the station because they had some questions about Michael. It's not a secret that I've known Michael since we were kids, so I really didn't think that much of the request. I thought maybe they were just trying to fill in some of the blanks in his life, you know?"

Rose nodded encouragingly.

"Michael pretty much kept to himself," Glenn said.

"So you didn't call a lawyer?" Mr. P. said.

Glenn shook his head. "I didn't. I didn't see why I needed to. I hadn't done anything wrong and I really thought the whole thing was just going to be routine." He picked up his coffee and then set it back down again. "I decided the best thing to do was to go right then and get it over with. So that's what I did."

"What happened?" I asked.

"Not exactly what I was expecting," he said. "I thought I'd be talking to someone in an office but instead they took me to what was clearly a room where they interrogate suspects. It had no windows, and honestly it felt a little claustrophobic."

Rose and Mr. P. exchanged a look.

"Detective Andrews came in and at first I still thought she'd ask me a few questions about Michael and that would be it. She thanked me for coming in and said the police were trying to get a better sense of who Michael was as a person."

"What did you tell her?" Rose asked.

"I said we were a lot closer when we were younger, but Michael was always way more introverted than any of my other friends. She wanted to know if I knew of any reason why Michael would have been down by the water."

Glenn turned his mug in a slow circle on the table. "I told her that made no sense to me. Michael had never been a very strong swimmer. The story he told me years ago was that when he was a kid some of his cousins threw him into the water off a dock. He almost drowned."

He looked at Rose and Mr. P. "Sarah already knows this part. That stretch of beach is where our friend Freddie died. You probably remember what happened."

Mr. P. nodded.

"I do," Rose said. "I'm sorry you had to go through something so horrible."

"Thank you," Glenn said. "That place was not somewhere I ever want to be and, as far as I knew, Michael felt the same way. Our lives changed forever that night and neither one of us wanted to relive that."

I gave an involuntary shiver and wrapped both hands around my mug. If I'd gone through what Glenn had I wouldn't have gone back to that place, either.

"I did ask if the police knew about Michael's allergy to sesame seeds," Glenn said. "I thought it was possible he'd eaten something and had a reaction. Detective Andrews said they already knew."

"Was that the only allergy he had?" Mr. P. asked.

Glenn nodded. "As far as I knew."

"Did all of Michael's friends know about his allergy?" Rose asked.

"Yes," Glenn said. "It wasn't a secret. Michael was very, very careful about what he ate. Before he got diagnosed he ended up in the ER more than once. It was right after we started hanging out together. I remember one time he was covered in hives and having trouble breathing. Turned out that was from the sesame seeds on a hamburger bun."

"Anaphylaxis," Rose said.

"Yes. It could have killed him. That's why he always carried an EpiPen. He had to change what he ate. No more everything bagels. No more hamburger buns with sesame seeds on them."

Glenn ducked his head for a moment and when he raised it again he looked directly at me. "Sarah, when I talked to you the other day I wasn't completely straight with you and I should have been. I'm sorry."

"Okay," I said slowly. "I'm guessing there's something you left out?"

"There is," he said. I could see the stress he was feeling etched in the lines on his face. "I might indirectly be the reason Michael was on that stretch of beach."

I felt my stomach lurch as though I were in a car that had suddenly and rapidly accelerated.

"I saw Michael the day that he died."

I hadn't been expecting that. "So why didn't you tell me?" I asked.

"Because we argued. We were on the street and more than one person heard and saw us."

"And when he turned up dead, at least one of those people went to the police," Mr. P. said.

Glenn nodded.

"What did you argue about?" Rose asked in her gentle way.

"The anniversary of Freddie's death is coming up soon. It's the same every year. I can't help thinking about everything that happened and it was the same for Michael. We hadn't spoken in probably six months and suddenly there he was, walking down the sidewalk toward me."

Once again he picked up his coffee cup and after a moment set it down without taking a drink. "He looked like hell, like he hadn't been sleeping, and I figured it was because of the time of year, because it was soon going to be fifteen years since Freddie died. Michael told me he'd done something he shouldn't have done and it was getting harder to live with himself. He said I was the only one he could talk to about this. I swear I didn't have a clue what he was talking about."

He looked from Rose to Mr. P. "Andrew Lewis went to prison for pushing Freddie off the rocks. She hit her head and drowned."

I remembered the wound on Michael's head.

"I recall there was some controversy about whether or not her death could have been accidental," Mr. P. said. He took off his glasses, took out the little cloth he carried in his shirt pocket and began to clean them. I knew he was still paying close attention to Glenn's story.

"Andrew always swore he was innocent," Glenn said, "but he thought the evidence was against him. He took some kind of plea."

"Did Michael tell you what he did that he shouldn't have?" I asked.

"He said that he saw someone else, someone other than Andrew, in a heated argument with Freddie right before she died. Someone who was shorter and thinner than Andrew. He didn't tell the police or any-one else what he'd seen."

I shook my head.

"I know," Glenn said. "I couldn't believe it, either. Michael had been drinking and he said he was afraid he'd be in trouble because he had also been driving with his sister in the car. I yelled at him right there on the street. How could he have kept something like that to himself all these years? I was so angry. Something like this might have created reasonable doubt at a trial. The police would have at least looked for the person. Andrew had always maintained he didn't hurt Freddie."

I looked at Rose. Her expression was somber.

"Did he say why he was telling you this now after so much time had passed?" Mr. P. asked.

"Andrew's grandmother died several weeks ago. She raised him. Michael couldn't stop thinking about all the time together they'd lost. It was eating at him." Glenn swallowed a couple of times. "I feel guilty that I thought Andrew killed Freddie and I hadn't be-lieved him when he insisted he didn't. So I told Mi-chael I'd give him until the end of the day on Friday to go to Andrew's lawyer and tell her what he'd just told me; otherwise I would take the story to Andrew's lawyer, the newspaper and anyone else who would listen. Michael said he needed to figure some things out and I said to get it done fast. I told all of this to the police."

He laid both hands on the table. "I didn't kill Mi-chael. I wouldn't have for any reason, no matter how angry I was at him, and I needed him alive to possibly clear Andrew's name. And that's what I told the police."

"And all they have is your word for why the two of you were arguing," I said.

"That's the problem," he said. "I don't think Michael said anything to anyone else."

"And they could argue your anger because he hadn't come forward sooner led you to lash out in the heat of the moment," Mr. P. said as he folded the little cloth and put it back in his pocket. "At a trial, Michael's story might have raised reasonable doubt in the jury's mind, but now it would take a lot more to help clear Andrew Lewis's name. And no one can give him back all the time he's spent behind bars."

"I swear I didn't kill Michael," Glenn said.

"We know that," I said. Rose and Mr. P. nodded their agreement.

"I want to make this right. I need you to find out who did kill him." Glenn looked at each of us in turn. "Please, will you help me?" he said.

I looked at Mr. P.

He looked at Rose.

"Of course we will," Rose said.

Glenn's shoulders sagged with relief. "So what do I do now?" he asked.

"You go back to work and you hold your head up because you didn't do anything wrong," Rose said firmly.

"Didn't I? I should have marched Michael over to that lawyer's office or the police or somewhere right then."

"And he could still be dead," Rose said. "His death

is not on your hands. The responsibility is on the person who killed him."

"Did they specifically tell you that Michael's death has been ruled a murder?" Mr. P. asked.

Glenn thought for a minute. "No, they didn't, but it was implied pretty strongly."

Mr. P. looked at me. "Sarah, I think Joshua's expertise would be helpful here."

Rose was already nodding.

"Glenn, do you know Josh Evans, the lawyer?" I said.

"Not that well, but he comes into the shop fairly regularly."

"When you get back there call Josh's office and take the first appointment they can give you."

Mr. P. got to his feet. "I have one of Joshua's cards." He got the business card from the inside pocket of his messenger bag and handed it to Glenn.

"Remember, take the first appointment Josh has available," I said, "and tell him everything you told us."

"He won't judge," Rose said. "And he's a very good lawyer."

I made a circle with one finger taking in myself, Rose and Mr. P. "The fact that we're all sitting here should tell you Josh is a very good lawyer."

Glenn smiled. "I'll call him the moment I get back to the shop."

"I think we all agree it would be best for Glenn not to talk to the police without Josh with him," Mr. P. said.

"But isn't that just going to make me look guilty?"

"On the contrary," Rose said. "It helps keep the

system honest, which means it works for everyone, guilty or innocent, rich or poor. Josh's job is to protect not just your rights, but the rights of everyone." Rose felt very strongly about how the justice system worked and you could hear that in her voice.

"Okay," Glenn said. He got to his feet. "Thank you. Please, just find out what happened."

"You have our word we will do our best," Mr. P. said.

"I'll walk you out," I said. We went out the back door and walked over to Glenn's truck.

"Rose is right," I said. "You didn't do anything wrong, so don't act like you did."

He smiled. "Thanks." He climbed into the truck and I walked back to the building.

Rose and Mr. P. were standing in the office.

I stopped in the doorway. "So now we have a case," I said.

Rose nodded. "Yes, now we have a case."

I was pretty sure Nick's head was going to explode.

Chapter 8

"Are we having a team meeting?" I asked. I didn't want to be the one who had to tell Nick what was going on.

"Do we really need to?" Rose said. "Everyone is going to want to help Glenn, even Nicolas."

"But we always get everyone together on the big cases," I said. "Besides I'm pretty sure nothing is official if we don't have cake." And I'd probably be stuck bringing Nick up to date. I narrowed my gaze at Rose. "You don't want to jinx Glenn's case, do you?"

Rose shook her head. "Fine," she said. "We'll call everyone together for an official meeting at twelve thirty because heaven forbid we jinx"—she made air quotes—"Glenn's case." She bustled out of the room saying over her shoulder, "The things you will do for cake, child."

"Thank you," I called after her.

Mr. P. smiled. "I do believe there's a spice cake in the staff room freezer," he said. Rose generally had a cake or a coffee cake or brownies in the freezer just for this kind of occasion.

I nodded. "I think you're right."

"And I believe Mac has cream cheese in his refrigerator. He gave me a little smear for my bagel on Saturday and I doubt he ate most of a container since then."

"So do I," I said.

"If he happens to have powdered sugar and a little vanilla perhaps Rose might make frosting for that spice cake."

I smiled. "Wouldn't that be delicious?"

He studied me for a moment. "Isn't spice cake with cream cheese frosting one of Nicolas's favorites?" A frown furrowed his forehead.

"I think you're right," I said. "Imagine that."

Mr. P. smiled. "Yes, imagine that."

I spent the rest of the morning in the shop working with a steady stream of customers. I sold the table and chairs from the window display and thought how Avery would say *I told you those chairs were a better choice.* Rose sold a box of dishes and an armoire that Mac managed to wedge into the back of a large SUV.

"Are you certain he's going to be able to get that thing out of his vehicle?" I asked Mac as the man who had bought the armoire pulled out of the parking lot.

Mac smiled. "Maybe fifty percent certain, sixty percent tops."

Avery arrived on time, wearing purple high-tops with her usual black T-shirt and black jeans, instead of her Dr. Martens. "What do you want me to do?" she asked.

"We're having a meeting," I said, "so the main thing I need you to do is watch the shop."

"Do we have a new case?" I noticed she'd said "we." So had Mac. So had I, for that matter.

"We do," I said, picking up the rubber mallet to hammer the lid back on a can of paint I'd just opened. I was looking for something to use on a small table.

"Does it have anything to do with the body you and Cleveland found?" She tipped her head to one side. The gesture made me think of Rose.

I nodded.

"So who is it?"

"Glenn," I said. I banged the lid in place and reached for another can of paint.

Avery rolled her eyes with typical teenage disdain. "Well, that's just stupid. Glenn couldn't kill anyone."

"I know," I said. Avery had a way of pointing out the obvious, which didn't always endear her to people. She was so like her grandmother.

"So that guy didn't drown by accident, someone killed him?"

"It looks that way."

"What's wrong with people?" she said.

I shrugged. "Sometimes I don't know."

I pried up the lid of the second paint can. It was a soft blue-gray shade. Avery leaned over my shoulder for a look. "What are you painting?" she asked.

"That little round table I bought from Teresa a couple of weeks ago."

"That'll work. We could put that green glass bowl on it once it's in the shop."

The 1950s vintage Art Deco bowl had been in and

out of the shop over the last six months and hadn't captured anyone's attention. Displaying it on the table might work. "Okay, this color it is." I smiled at her. "Thanks."

"No problem," she said.

I put the lid back on the can. Hopefully I could start painting after lunch.

"Are we having cake?" Avery asked.

"I think so," I said. I was hoping Nick could be mollified by a big slice. Assuming he showed up for the meeting. "I'll make sure you get a piece."

"Can I move some things around in the shop?"

"I don't know. Can you?" I asked.

She made a face. "You sound like Charlotte."

I gave her a big smile in return. "That's not a bad thing."

"Fine," she said in an aggrieved voice. "*May* I move some things around in the shop?"

"Yes, you may," I said. Avery had a good eye for color and design and whatever she did would look good and, just as important, catch customers' attention. "And I got more teacups so you can do more plantings."

"I need more actual plants," she said, leaning back against the workbench. Elvis appeared from somewhere and jumped up to nuzzle her shoulder. "And I'm pretty low on potting soil."

"I'll bring both tomorrow," I said.

"After the meeting *may* I clean out the storage area under the stairs?" She smiled at Elvis and scratched behind his ear. He started to purr.

I nodded. "That's an excellent idea. Things have

gotten out of control under there lately." I held up one hand. "Yes, I know it's pretty much my fault."

"Yeah, it pretty much is," she said.

Charlotte and Liz came in the back door. "There you are," Liz said. "What's this foolishness about Glenn McNamara?"

"He's the new client," I said. I banged the lid on the paint can and set it aside.

"I know that," Liz said. "What I don't know is why."

"You'll get all your questions answered in five minutes," I said. "Mr. P. is in the office."

"Fine," she said. She headed for the Angels' office, the heels of her lavender pumps clicking across the floor. "But I don't see why you can't answer my questions right now."

Avery was looking in the box of teacups I bought. "The police think Glenn killed the dead man that Sarah and Cleveland found, probably because he was yelling at the guy outside the bakery that morning."

"Now that wasn't so hard, was it?" Liz said over her shoulder before she disappeared into the office.

I turned to Avery. "How did you know about Glenn arguing with Michael Norris? And how did you know who Michael Norris was?"

"Well, duh, I knew they were arguing because I was there. And as for who the guy was, I didn't know then, but Nonna gets the newspaper and I do read. I saw his picture."

I stared at her for a minute. "What do you mean, you were there?" None of this made any sense.

"Greg and I were there. At the bakery. We went for breakfast before school 'cause they open early. They have a really good breakfast sandwich." Two spots of color appeared on her cheeks. "Once in a while I like a little bacon."

Avery was a vegan some of the time with exceptions for Rose's sausage rolls and Charlotte's turkey and gravy, and now, apparently for Glenn's breakfast sandwiches. Greg was her boyfriend of sorts. They'd been on and off and now on for several months.

"You can have all the bacon you want as far as I'm concerned," I said.

"I have it maybe, *maybe* twice a year," she said. "Everyone else here eats bacon more than that."

I held up one hand. "Missing the point here. When I told you Glenn was our new client, why didn't you tell me what you saw?"

She shrugged. "I figured if he was our new client"—I noticed her choice of words once again—"that he probably already told you."

"He did."

"Then I don't see what the problem is."

I pressed my lips together because as much as I loved Avery, her teenager logic made me want to scream sometimes.

Charlotte very wisely stepped in. "It's not a problem," she said "But you can give us a different perspective as an observer. What did you see?"

Avery slid her bracelets up and down her arm as she thought about Charlotte's question. "Glenn wasn't expecting to see the guy," she said.

I opened my mouth to say something but Charlotte silenced me with a look. "What makes you say that?" she asked.

"Well, see, once he opens he takes the broom and goes and sweeps the front steps and the bit of sidewalk. I don't know why he doesn't do that before he opens. Anyway he was sweeping and the dead guy—I mean, he wasn't dead then, obviously—came up the sidewalk. Greg and I were sitting by the window and could see Glenn's face and he looked surprised."

"How did the other man look?"

Elvis butted Avery's arm and she picked him up and began to stroke his fur. "Serious," she said. "And nervous. He was what Nonna would call all twitchy."

I stifled a smile because Liz had no patience for people who couldn't stand still.

"He kept shifting from one foot to the other and he didn't keep his hands still, either. He had a backpack over one shoulder and he kept fiddling with the strap."

"What happened after that?" Charlotte said. No wonder she'd been such a well-liked principal. She had an infinite supply of patience.

Avery shrugged. "I don't know. I was eating my sandwich and Greg was talking about his chemistry exam that he thought he flunked but of course he didn't. The next time I looked, Glenn was yelling at that guy. I couldn't hear the words, but his face was red and his hands were going everywhere. The other guy, Norris, was mad, but he wasn't as loud. He had his arms crossed and he didn't back away when Glenn was yelling. Finally he just walked away, but not like he was afraid of Glenn. He was all kind of stiff, like he was mad but didn't want to show it." She shrugged. "That's pretty much it."

"That helps," Charlotte said. "Thank you."

I nodded. "It does help. I'm sorry I snapped at you."

"No problem," Avery said. "I get that you just want to help Glenn."

Charlotte touched my arm. "We better get in there before Rose comes down and we end up in the doghouse."

"Good point," I said. "Come get me if you need help," I told Avery, "and I'll save you a piece of cake."

Charlotte and I headed down to the office while Avery and Elvis went into the shop. "Is Nick coming?" I asked.

"I don't know," Charlotte said. "I haven't talked to him."

"I think Rose might have called him."

"Doesn't Alfred have Nick's proxy?" she said as she took her jacket off.

"I'm not sure, but it may have been revoked. Nick claimed it was given under duress."

Charlotte smiled. "Well, it's not like he's going to give it to his mother."

I took her jacket and hung it on the back of a chair. "Don't feel bad, he wouldn't give it to me, either."

Rose and Mr. P. arrived then with the tea and cake, which I noticed had fluffy white frosting. Perfect. Mac came behind them with two cups of coffee. He handed one to me and set the other on the table.

"That's for Nick if he shows up," he said. "I'm going to help Avery. A van of bingo players just showed up." He handed me a piece of paper with his name scrawled on it. "You now have my proxy. Use it wisely."

I grinned. "The power is already going to my head."

Mac slipped out, passing Nick in the doorway. I caught his eye and he came to join me.

I pointed at the coffee on the table. "That's yours," I said.

"Thanks," he said, reaching behind me for the mug.

"Thank Mac," I said. "He brought it for you."

"Yeah, where was he going?"

I took a sip of my own coffee. "To help Avery, but I have his proxy."

Nick shook his head. "No good will come of that."

I stuck my tongue out at him and he laughed.

Before Nick could say anything else Rose clapped her hands and we all looked at her. She smiled. Then she glanced at me and said, "We're having this meeting because we have a new client, Glenn McNamara."

"The police can't possibly think Glenn killed someone," Liz said. She looked pointedly at Nick.

He held up both hands. "I don't know what the police are thinking. I swear. I haven't talked to Michelle or anyone else so far today. I can tell you that the autopsy has been done, but that's all I know. There should be a preliminary report sometime late this afternoon."

"Do you know what it's going to say?" Rose asked.

Nick shrugged. "I don't, but I will concede that if the police really are looking at Glenn as a suspect, then it doesn't sound like they think Michael Norris's death was an accident."

Liz looked at me. "What do you think? You were there. Do you think the man was murdered?"

I hadn't expected anyone to ask that question. I

took a breath and let it out slowly, trying to figure out what to say. "I don't know. But based on what Glenn told us this morning, it does sound like he's a suspect, which points toward murder, not an accident."

"But why do the police even think Glenn is involved?" Liz asked.

Mr. P. explained about the two men having had a loud argument on the street the day Michael Norris died. "Several people heard and saw them," he said.

"Including Avery, it turns out," I added. With the exception of Charlotte they all looked at me in surprise. Charlotte nodded in agreement.

"Then what's the point of talking about this any longer?" Liz said. "I vote yes to taking on Glenn's case."

"I do as well," Charlotte said.

"I'm a yes and so is Mac," I said. I waved the piece of paper he'd given me in the air. "I have his proxy."

"I agree as well," Rose said.

Mr. P. nodded. "So do I."

We all looked at Nick. "Does it really matter what I think?" he asked. I had expected him to tell Rose what a bad idea this all was, but he hadn't.

"Of course it does," Rose said.

"Okay. So what if I voted no?"

Rose brushed off the front of her apron. "Then I would want to know why. Maybe you saw something the rest of us missed. Maybe you know something about Glenn that we don't. Maybe you saw the significance of some detail that none of us caught." She looked at him, head tipped to one side like a quizzical little finch.

"Are you voting no, Nicolas?" Mr. P. asked. Nick's mouth twisted to one side for a moment like he was chewing on something. Rose continue to watch him and I fought the urge to hip-check him into a chair.

"I don't like this," he finally said, "but nothing I say is going to stop all of you, and the truth is, I agree with everyone else. I just don't believe Glenn would kill anyone. I vote yes."

Chapter 9

Rose beamed at him. "Excellent." She looked at Liz. "We need to know all the gossip about the murder of Freddie Black fifteen years ago. It's possible the two cases are connected."

Liz stretched out one arm and looked at her perfectly manicured hands. "I believe a visit to Phantasy is in order."

Phantasy was her niece Elspeth's spa, and a great place to hear all of the North Harbor gossip.

Rose turned to Charlotte next. "It would be very helpful to hear what Clayton knows as well."

Charlotte nodded.

"Alf will talk to Merton and see what the neighbors have to say about Michael Norris." She looked at me. "Will you talk to Michelle and see if you can find out why on earth they're looking at Glenn, please?"

"I can't promise she'll tell me anything," I said.

"Do your best," she said in her former middle school teacher voice. "I'll talk to Josh Evans and see if we should be working for him and not Glenn directly."

"Don't I get an assignment?" Nick asked.

Rose nodded. "Yes, you do. I want to know how Michael Norris died."

"There won't be any final report until all the testing is complete. That can take a while."

"I know that," Rose said.

"When the final report is ready you can pay the fee and request a copy," Nick said.

She smiled at him. "Oh, I know that, as well," she said, "but you can tell me a lot faster. As you pointed out, I could request a copy of the report and get the same information so you aren't breaching any rules."

He shrugged. "All right. I'll see what I can do. No promises."

Rose looked around the room at all of us. "Any questions?" No one said anything. "Fine," she said. "Let's get started."

I cut a slice of cake and handed it to Nick with a fork. I had a fork of my own and swiped a bite from his plate. "Oh, that's good," I said with a little swoon.

Nick took a much bigger bite and gave a little groan of pleasure.

"So how long will the autopsy report take?" I asked, licking a tiny bit of frosting off the back of my fork.

"The final report could take several weeks," he said. "There are various tests that need to be done. But there could be some indication of cause of death already." He took another bite of cake. Then his expression changed. He held up the plate. "Is that what this is? You're trying to bribe me to tell you what the preliminary report says?"

I swiped another forkful of cake while he was distracted. "Good grief!" I said. "Give me credit for coming up with a better bribe than that." I managed to snag yet another forkful before he moved the plate out of my reach. "Though I will concede that as bribes go, this would be a delicious one."

He gave me a look. I gave him one right back. We'd been doing that since we were kids.

"First of all, the cake was in the freezer because Rose keeps an emergency cake in case we have a last-minute meeting," I said. "Second, she put frosting on it because Mac happened to have cream cheese because we'd had bagels and because Rose *always* puts cream cheese frosting on her spice cake, but if you're so certain I'm trying to wheedle information out of you, then fine, give me the cake and I'll finish it." I tried to take the plate from him and he held it up over my head. I folded my arms and glared at him, deciding that jumping and trying to grab the plate was probably a bit undignified.

"Okay, look, I'm sorry," he said, lowering his arm.

I leaned against the table next to him. "It's okay," I said. "It's just that it was bad enough thinking that someone died feet away from Memphis's house and no one heard anything and to now find out that Michelle thinks Glenn, of all people, had something to do with it." I shook my head. "I'd give you the whole darn cake for a bribe if I thought it would help Glenn."

Nick held out the plate and I speared another bite. "Thanks," I said.

"Look," he said. "Michelle is just doing her job. She has to go where the evidence leads her and if the evidence says Norris was murdered and there's a connection to Glenn and his business, then that's the direction she has to go no matter what her personal opinion of Glenn may be. She can't play favorites and she can't tell you anything even if she wants to."

I sighed. "I know you're right, but I still need to talk to her, if only to let her know the Angels are on the case."

"Fair enough," he said.

"Can you really get that information that Rose wants faster than she can?" I asked.

"Yeah, I probably can. And I could probably talk to whichever medical examiner's investigator worked the case and ask a few *very general* questions."

I smiled. "Hey, thanks," I said.

Nick ate the last bite of cake and set the plate on the table. "I have to get going. Try to keep this motley group on the straight and narrow."

"If you wanted me to do that, you should have let me have more of the cake," I said with a grin.

He just shook his head and went to say hello to his mother and Liz. I watched him hug both of them and talk for a moment. Then he went to speak to Rose. I had no idea what he was saying, but based on her smile I was guessing it was praise for the cake. Finally he said something to Mr. P., who nodded and gestured at his computer. Then Nick left.

I straightened up and went over to Rose. Charlotte passed me. "I'm going to check on Avery and Mac," she said.

"I'll be there in a minute," I said.

Mr. P. and Liz were talking about something I couldn't eavesdrop on from where I was standing. "The preliminary autopsy report points to Michael Norris having been murdered," I told Rose. "And there's more than just the argument between Michael and Glenn that makes Glenn a suspect."

"You got Nicolas to tell you that?" Rose asked.

"Not exactly," I said. "He let it slip that the evidence points to Norris's death not being an accident and that Glenn and *his business* are connected."

"Very good," Rose said approvingly.

"Avery mentioned when she saw Michael Norris he was carrying a backpack. It could be the one I saw on the beach. And when we were down at the jam Nick admitted that there were picnic things inside, although he wouldn't say the backpack was Norris's."

"I think we can safely make that assumption now," Rose said.

"I've been assuming that injury to Michael Norris's head was what killed him," I said, "but maybe it wasn't. Do you think someone could have used Michael Norris's food allergy to try to murder him?"

"It's certainly possible, but how would the medical examiner know it was murder versus an accident?"

"Good point," I said.

Liz and Mr. P. were still talking.

"I'd better go see what's happening in the shop," I said.

"I'll walk you." Rose picked up the cake plate. There were two slices left. She used a fork to slide one piece onto a napkin and handed it to me, along with the fork. "For Mac," she said sternly.

I smiled. "Thank you."

We started for the shop.

"Nick thought I was using the cake to bribe him," I said.

"Were you?"

"Like I told him, I have no control over what kind of cake you put in the freezer."

Rose nodded. "That's true, because if you did, all that would ever be there is chocolate."

I grinned at her. "It is the finest of the flavors."

"And for the record," Rose said, "you were in the staff room when I put that cake in the freezer and I told you it was a spice cake."

Rose didn't miss a trick. "Fine. I knew there was spice cake in the freezer, which is one of Nick's favorites, and I also knew that Mac had cream cheese in his refrigerator, which is a pretty rare occurrence. But I would never try to bribe Nick." I gave Rose a sly smile. "I might, however, try to get his guard down a little with a piece of his favorite cake, which is not the same thing."

Rose smiled. "Well, isn't it lucky that I made the spice cake in the first place and that you remembered it was in the freezer and insisted on a meeting. And of course that Mac just happened to have cream cheese. I love it when a plan comes together." She patted my cheek, gathered Avery and they headed upstairs with the last slice of cake.

Mac and Charlotte were standing in a bare spot on the floor. I handed him the piece of cake I was holding.

"Thank you," he said. He took a bite and nodded his approval.

I looked around. "Where's the china cabinet?" I asked.

"Avery sold it," Mac said.

"But it wasn't even in here for a full day," I said.

Mac smiled. "Avery could sell snow shovels in a heat wave. What do you want to bring in next?"

I smoothed a hand back over my hair. "I don't know." I'd been trying to clear out some of the items in the workshop that had been sitting around for a while. I hadn't expected the china cabinet to sell so fast and I had no idea what to bring in next. "Charlotte, would you go look and see if anything grabs you? Please?"

"Of course," Charlotte said. "I'll be right back." She headed for the back door and I turned to Mac, who had already eaten half the piece of cake with just a couple of forkfuls.

"What made you buy bagels and cream cheese last weekend?" I asked.

"Oh, I didn't," he said. "Rose gave them to me. She got bagels for Alfred from the farmers' market and gave me half and the cream cheese as well."

I looked at the stairs and thought about Rose smiling and saying she loved it when a plan comes together. I wondered if ultimately the person who'd gotten played was me.

Charlotte came back and suggested we move in a matching dressing table and tall chest of drawers along with a huge chair bench that had been in and out of the shop twice in the last six months. It was a very large piece of furniture made of oak and probably dated from the late 1890s with lots of carved details. It was more than five feet high and four and a half feet wide. It had come from a house we had cleared out after its owner, a former minister and onetime circus clown, had died at age ninety-eight. It had certainly been the most intriguing home we had ever worked in.

"Are you sure about the bench?" I asked.

"It would be perfect in any of the bed-and-breakfasts in town," Charlotte said. "All we need is someone who is willing to invest in a beautiful piece of antique furniture."

"And four really strong people to move it," Mac added.

"I think Greg is meeting Avery at the end of the day," Charlotte said. "He'll help."

I spent the afternoon in the shop helping customers while Avery got the under-the-stairs storage area organized and Charlotte rearranged things a little to accommodate the bedroom furniture and the chair bench. I ended up selling two guitars, one to a teenage girl whose face lit up the moment I tuned it and handed it to her.

"I like to see that," Charlotte said, putting an arm around my shoulders.

"Me too," I said.

Avery and the girl talked for a minute. "She goes to my school," Avery said once she was gone, carrying the guitar as if it were a treasure chest. "She's really smart."

"That's something the two of you have in common," Charlotte said.

Avery rolled her eyes, but I also saw a hint of her smile flash across her face.

At the end of the day Greg showed up and was happy to help move the bench, commenting that it wasn't as heavy as it looked, which made me smile because *I* was thinking it was *a lot* heavier than it looked. We got the monstrosity into the shop and Charlotte said she'd dress it up in the morning and give it a good dusting.

"I might have a couple of seat cushions in the attic that will work," she added.

Avery and Greg left together. Charlotte decided to walk home because it was so nice. Mac was going out to work on the boat. Mr. P. and Rose drove with Elvis and me.

"I'll call Michelle tonight," I said, "because I didn't have a chance this afternoon."

"I'm having coffee with Merton in the morning," Mr. P. said from the backseat, where he and Elvis were having a conversation about support socks. The cat seemed for them, while Mr. P. appeared to be on the fence.

"I'm meeting with Josh in the morning as well," Rose said. "I should take him some cookies."

"We're making progress."

"Perhaps more than you think," Mr. P. said. "I had a conversation with Memphis earlier this afternoon. It occurred to me that he may have seen some of what the police were doing."

Rose turned to look at him. "And did he?"

"Yes, he did. He admitted to walking out to the top of the embankment and watching for a while."

I glanced in the rearview mirror. Mr. P. was smiling at me. "Rosie told me what you learned from Nicolas. I may have an idea what the connection is with Glenn and the bakery."

"I'd love to hear that," I said.

"Memphis saw them going through the backpack. He says there was a container of carrots, a Mason jar of what looked to be hummus. And a small bag of those big soft bread pretzels that Glenn makes."

"Are you sure about the hummus?" Rose asked.

"No, my dear, I'm not," he said, "but I am about the pretzels."

"Do you think the police believe Glenn tried to use Michael Norris's allergy against him?" I asked.

"Yes," he said. "I do."

Chapter 10

"That makes no sense," Rose said. "First of all, Glenn isn't that stupid. Why would he use food from his own bakery to kill Michael Norris? He had to know he'd be the first person the police would look at. And second, he doesn't even sell containers of hummus."

"I don't disagree," Mr. P. said, "but I do believe it is the avenue the police are pursuing. And in their defense, even though he doesn't sell hummus, it doesn't mean Glenn doesn't have any in the kitchen. Some people like it as a substitute for mayonnaise."

Rose turned in her seat to look at him. "We have to find out if Mr. Norris died from anaphylaxis."

"I think that would be very helpful information to have," he said.

"Is the rest of this conversation going to require me to wear the cone of silence?" I asked. Out of the corner of my eye I could see Rose was frowning.

"My goodness, I don't think we need to go to those

extremes," she said. "It seems to me that's the kind of information Josh might be able to get."

"That's a good idea," I said. I glanced in the mirror again and the thoughtful expression on Mr. P.'s face told me that he was likely trying to come up with a way to find out what we wanted to know if Josh didn't come through. I decided it was a good time to change the subject.

"Rose, what do you remember about Freddie Black's death?" I asked.

"I remember when it happened," she said. "It was such a shock, but I didn't recall a lot of the details so I checked the newspaper archives a couple of days ago to refresh my memory."

I stopped to let a woman walking a huge Newfoundland dog cross the street. The dog turned to look at us, wagged its tail and almost seemed to smile. "So what did you find out?" I said.

"In the beginning everyone assumed her death was an accident. They were down by the water, having a party. There was some drinking, of course. The police thought that Freddie had gone out onto the breakwater and slipped on the wet rocks. When she fell she hit her head, then slipped into the water and drowned."

"So what changed their minds?" I asked.

"A couple of things," Mr. P. said. "First of all Freddie Black had grown up in the area. She'd been all over the beach and those rocks since she was a child. And her hobby happened to be rock climbing. To her family it didn't make sense she'd have slipped and lost her footing so easily."

"But it was a party and people were drinking."

"True. But Freddie was a bit of an outlier. She didn't drink."

I glanced at Rose. She was nodding in agreement. "Then someone came forward and said they saw Freddie and Andrew Lewis arguing," she said. "According to the witness Freddie walked away from Andrew and he followed her out onto the rocks."

"But this witness didn't see them struggling or see him push her into the water?"

"No, he didn't," Rose said.

"The witness was a young woman looking for somewhere to be alone with a young man," Mr. P. said. "Their attention was otherwise engaged."

I nodded. "Okay, I get it."

"A day later a second witness corroborated the story. He saw the same thing: Freddie Black and Andrew Lewis arguing, Freddie walking away and Andrew Lewis following her. No one seems to know the name of that second witness."

We were almost home. "So what was Andrew Lewis's story?" I asked.

"He admitted that he and Freddie were arguing," Rose said, "but he claimed that when she walked away from him, he went in the other direction, back to the party. He insisted he didn't follow her out onto the breakwater. The next time he looked he didn't see Freddie and he just assumed she was somewhere else on the beach. It was more than twenty minutes later that someone caught sight of her body in the water. A couple of people did CPR and the paramedics came, but it was too late."

I shook my head. "Not a very nice way to die."

"No, it was not," Mr. P. agreed.

"So Andrew Lewis took a plea deal."

"An Alford plea."

"That's basically pleading guilty but insisting you're innocent," I said.

"You have the gist of it," Mr. P. said. "An Alford plea allows a defendant to enter a guilty plea to the charge, but still maintain their innocence. What they're saying is that there is enough evidence for a jury to find them guilty, so it's in their best interests to plead guilty."

"Do you know what evidence there was?"

He smiled. "I may have done a little digging," he said. "There were the two witnesses. Everyone seemed to think Andrew Lewis was the last person seen with Freddie. No one remembered seeing anyone with her after they argued. In his defense it was getting dark and they had all been drinking, so the timeline was a bit fuzzy."

"It doesn't seem like enough to have gotten a conviction," I said.

"It seems this wasn't the first argument Freddie and Andrew had had. They were both grad students and they had different opinions on how their respective tutorials should be run. The professor who was supervising both of them gave them a lot of latitude."

"But there has to be more than that," I said.

"There is," Mr. P. said. "The police found a St. Christopher medal on the rocks where they believed Freddie went into the water. It belonged to Andrew Lewis. It had originally been his late father's. The police theory was that Freddie pulled it from his neck when he pushed her. His attorney claimed Andrew had lost it earlier while he was swimming and it had washed up on the rocks when the tide came in." He cleared his throat. "And there were also bruises on her body."

"Bruises? Where?"

"One on her right wrist as if someone had grabbed her arm. The other right below her collarbone as though she had been hit, either with the heel of a hand or a fist."

I blew out a breath and pulled into the driveway. "Okay, Glenn says that Michael Norris saw someone else arguing with Freddie. Would that have been enough to raise reasonable doubt?"

"I'm not certain," Rose said, "but that's something I'll ask Josh when I talk to him."

Rose and Mr. P. headed down the hall to her apartment and I unlocked the door to mine. I made a big bowl of spaghetti for supper with sauce I'd made myself and Elvis had cat food, although I think he would have preferred the spaghetti.

After he had finished eating he made his way into the bedroom to get settled in to watch *Jeopardy!* I stalled by running the vacuum around the kitchen and living room and shaking the mat by the front door outside, but finally I picked up the phone to call Michelle. No surprise, I got her voice mail. I left a short message asking her to call me and left it at that.

I got out the quilt I'd bought on the weekend and used my stain remover solution on one small stain on the back of it. I left the quilt spread out in the bathtub while the stain remover did its work for a few minutes. As I got to my feet I heard my phone. It was Michelle.

"Hi," she said. "I got your message. I'm guessing your call has something to do with Michael Norris."

"Good guess," I said, dropping onto the sofa. "It does."

"I haven't eaten yet, have you?" she asked.

"I have," I said.

"Darn. I was going to ask if you wanted to join me for supper. We said we were going to try to get together."

"Hey, I've got spaghetti sauce I made, which is pretty good, if I say so myself. How about I make you supper?"

Michelle hesitated, then she said, "You know, the truth is I'd like that."

I smiled even though she couldn't see me. "So would I."

"Okay, I should be there in about twenty minutes."

We ended the call and I went to deal with the quilt. Then I set a place for Michelle at the kitchen table. I grated a little mozzarella cheese because I had no Parmesan, and lastly I put a pot of water on to boil.

Michelle was right on time.

"I'm glad you came," I said, giving her a hug.

"So am I," she said. "It's been a long day. You have no idea how good it is to not have to make a decision about what I want to eat, let alone cook it."

I started the pasta and turned the heat on low under the sauce. Michelle leaned against the counter. She was wearing a gold shirt and a darker caramel blazer over black trousers with her hair loose just brushing her shoulders.

"I'm guessing your call had something to do with Glenn McNamara," she said.

"Yeah, it did," I said. "I'm not sure how to say this, but I've been struggling with the idea that you could even think Glenn McNamara would hurt anyone."

"C'mon. You know I can't make decisions based on my personal feelings."

I leaned over and stirred the sauce.

"Nick reminded me of that."

She smiled. "I'll have to remember to thank him."

"I know how things look," I said. "Glenn arguing on the street with Michael Norris the same day Cleveland finds Michael's body in the water."

She shook her head. "Alfred Peterson is good," she said, an edge of grudging respect in the voice.

I shook my head. "Alfred didn't do anything. Avery was there." I paused. "And I talked to Glenn."

Michelle laughed and looked up at the ceiling as though there were some kind of answers to all of this up there. "I should have seen it coming. He hired Rose and her band of merry detectives, didn't he? *That's* why you called."

"It is," I said.

"All I was doing was talking to Glenn. He was free to leave anytime he wanted to."

I stirred the sauce again. "I know that, but you didn't ask him down to the police station to talk without a reason. I know you don't have a final autopsy report, but you wouldn't have called Glenn in first thing Monday morning if you didn't have some reason to believe Michael Norris's death was *not* accidental. You don't operate that way." I checked the spaghetti and decided it needed about another minute.

"So what was I supposed to do? Not follow a lead? I can't give preferential treatment to Glenn just because I like his blueberry muffins. When he didn't want to answer any more questions I didn't try to stop him from leaving. And he always had the option to call a lawyer. Did it occur to you that maybe what I was trying to do was eliminate Glenn as a suspect?"

I checked the pasta a second time and it was ready. I put the spaghetti in a big white stoneware bowl and topped it with sauce, setting it and the grated mozzarella on the table.

"Enjoy," I said to Michelle, who hesitated and then sat down.

I cleared my throat. "I'm sorry," I said. "It didn't cross my mind that you might have been trying to rule Glenn out as a suspect. But it should have."

"It never does occur to people," she said. "In the end my job is to figure out what happened, to look at each piece of evidence and see how it fits with every other piece. Not to protect anyone's feelings and the sauce is terrific. Did you really make it?"

I nodded. "Think of it as an apology with cheese." I really was sorry. I had underestimated her.

Michelle grinned. "I didn't think you would ever learn how to cook."

I laughed. "Neither did anyone else. Neither did I!"

I pulled out the chair across from her and sat down. "In the interest of full disclosure Rose thinks there's a connection between Michael Norris's death and the death of Freddie Black."

She looked up at me. "She might be right."

"What do you mean, she might be right?"

"I mean there were two deaths in the same area, involving the same people. It would be pretty dumb not to at least consider the possibility that they might be connected."

I rubbed my forehead with one hand. "Okay, now I have a headache," I said. "You and Rose looking at things from the same perspective. I may have fallen into an alternate universe."

"We've agreed before . . . on something . . . I think." She smiled. "Anyway you know what they say. 'Great minds think alike.'"

"I feel obliged to remind you that the rest of that quote goes, 'though fools seldom differ,'" I said.

Elvis padded into the kitchen, made his way over to Michelle's chair and meowed.

"Hello, Elvis," she said.

He launched himself onto her lap.

"Elvis, get down from there!" I said, reaching over to pick him up.

"It's okay," Michelle said. "I don't mind."

"He'll get cat hair all over your shirt."

She laughed. "Oh, I've had way worse on this shirt."

Elvis turned to look at me.

"You have no manners," I said.

He gave me a smug look in return. Michelle stroked his fur and he settled happily on her lap as she finished the last bites of her spaghetti.

"You're not going to tell me how Michael Norris died, are you?" I said.

"You know I can't do that."

I propped my elbows on the table since Liz wasn't here to ask me if I'd been raised by wolves. "Couldn't we play red light, green light like we did when we were kids and if I get close to the right answer all you have to say is 'green light.'"

Michelle grinned. "No, we can't do that, either."

"But his death wasn't an accident."

She looked down at the cat. "She doesn't give up, does she?"

Elvis murped in agreement, much to her amusement.

She looked up at me again. "Sarah, you saw the body."

I felt my stomach clench at the memory. I nodded.

"And you were there on that stretch of sand."

"I was."

"Then draw your own conclusions." She smiled. "Could we talk about something else? Please?"

I nodded. I wanted our friendship to be about more than whatever case she and the Angels had in common at any given time. "Tell me about the house," I said.

After months and months of searching she had finally found a house to buy. Her first house. The closing was in a couple of weeks.

I held up both hands. "I'm available for pretty much anything."

"Good," she said, "because I'm going to need a lot of help."

We talked about the layout of the small house and what colors Michelle liked.

"My best advice from my experience with this house is do what you need to do to make it habitable—which I'm guessing won't be too much—and then live in the house for a few months and figure out what you like and what you don't like. If I'd followed that advice the kitchen would not have changed color three times in the first six weeks."

We talked for a good half hour and finally Michelle said she'd better get going. She glanced at the dishes.

"Go home," I said. "I can do those. Elvis will help."

Right on cue he meowed loudly.

Michelle laughed. "I don't know if that was a yes or a no." She set Elvis on the floor and hugged me. "Thank you for the food and the conversation."

"I'm glad you came," I said. "We have to do this again now that I can make more than toast."

"Tell Rose and Alfred to keep me in the loop and try not to break any laws."

"I'll pass on the message but beyond that, I make no promises," I said.

Michelle said good night and left.

"I was hoping we might learn a little more about Michael Norris's death other than Glenn may or may not be a suspect and Norris may or may not have been murdered," I said to Elvis.

He jumped up onto one of the stools at the counter.

I looked at him. "Michelle said to draw my own conclusions. How is that supposed to help me? Or is it?
What did she mean?"

The cat gave me a blank look and began to wash
his face. It seemed he didn't know, either.

Chapter 11

Rose and Mr. P. drove in with Elvis and me in the morning. Elvis decided to sit in front with Rose and me and make little grumbling noises about my driving all the way to the shop.

I told them about my conversation with Michelle. "I feel even more convinced that the police think Michael Norris was murdered. And I have no idea what Michelle meant when she told me to draw my own conclusions."

"I think she meant exactly what she said," Rose offered. "You're smart. Think about what you saw and what you've learned and decide what it's all telling you."

"That's the problem," I said. "I don't know what it's all telling me. I saw a body. I saw a backpack. I know Michael Norris has a connection to a death that happened close to fifteen years ago. I know he and Glenn had an argument. I got nothing." My voice was getting louder and more agitated.

Rose put a hand on my arm. "You're trying too hard."

"I'm not sure I'm trying hard enough."

"To extend the puzzle analogy, try not to force the pieces to fit," Mr. P. said.

I smiled. "I've decided for Christmas this year I'm going to buy you a puzzle I saw last time I was in Camden. It was bees, nothing but dozens and dozens of bees in a hive. And then when you're working on it I'll be able to say, 'Try not to force the pieces to fit.'"

"That sounds like a challenge," he said. "Thank you. I'm sure I'd enjoy it."

I looked in the mirror to find him smiling at me. I had a feeling he was yanking my chain, but with Alfred Peterson it was hard to tell.

"Maybe Alf and I will come up with something from our respective meetings this morning," Rose said.

"I can drive you," I said.

"Thank you," Mr. P. said, "but we already have something arranged with Mac."

I looked at him again as I turned into the parking lot. "I think you just like driving around in Mac's truck."

He smiled. "I can't really deny that."

Charlotte was waiting for us by the back door. "I talked to Clayton last night and learned a little bit more about Glenn's friends," she said. "I don't know if any of it will be helpful."

Mr. P. looked at his watch. "We have some time. Perhaps a brief gathering in the office in five minutes is in order."

"I think that's an excellent idea," Rose said.

When I got to the top of the stairs Mac was just coming out of the staff room with two cups of coffee.

He smiled. "You're early," he said, handing me one of the cups and leaning in to kiss me.

"Thank you," I said, taking a sip and sighing with happiness. "We're having a brief meeting in the Angels' office in just a few minutes so Charlotte can tell us what she learned about Glenn's friends."

"Do you think they're connected to Michael Norris's death?"

"Rose certainly does, and I'm inclined to agree with her."

"Is this an official meeting if there's no cake?" Mac asked.

I swatted his arm and he laughed.

Charlotte came up the stairs. "The kettle is about to boil," he said.

She smiled at him and then looked at me. "This one is a prize."

"Yes, he is," I agreed.

Mac frowned. "*This* one? Does that mean there were ones that weren't?"

"No comment," I said firmly.

Charlotte got a thoughtful expression on her face. A very fake, thoughtful expression. "What about the guy with the Elvis sideburns?"

I gave her a look. "We agreed we would never speak of those sideburns."

Charlotte patted Mac's shoulder. "We'll talk later," she stage-whispered and went into the staff room.

"No, you won't," I called after her.

Once Charlotte brought the tea down we settled at the long table in the office.

"Glenn had been friends with Michael Norris since junior high," Charlotte began. "They were part of a tight group of friends that included Andrew Lewis and Freddie Black. Michael was a year younger than the others because he skipped a grade in elementary school."

I remembered Glenn saying he and Michael had been friends since the eighth grade.

"You already know that almost fifteen years ago all four of them were at a July Fourth party on the beach behind Clayton's property. He wasn't home. It wasn't the first party Glenn had had there, but there had never been any trouble and Clayton admits he pretty much turned a blind eye. Freddie Black drowned after apparently being pushed into the water and hitting her head. Andrew Lewis went to prison. Clayton said that Andrew and Freddie were grad students for the same professor and from what he'd seen, they were always arguing about something."

"Did Clayton say why they argued so much?" Mr. P. asked.

Charlotte nodded. "I wondered the same thing myself. Apparently Freddie was very much a follow-the-rules kind of person. She'd been raised by a single mother and had worked incredibly hard to get her undergraduate degree. She had strong opinions and she wasn't afraid to say what she thought. She had no time for anyone who was slacking off."

I'd had help from my parents, but I'd also had to work hard to get my degree. They'd had both Liam and me in college at the same time. I remembered feeling a little resentful of my friends whose parents were footing the whole thing.

Charlotte took a sip of her tea. "Andrew, it seems, was a lot more relaxed and Freddie seemed to think he was just enabling laziness in the students in the tutorial section he was responsible for. She thought he marked too leniently and was lax about deadlines. Clayton said Glenn told him Freddie had threatened to go to their supervising professor because Andrew routinely let students turn in their assignments late, which violated the professor's rules about deadlines and could have gotten Andrew into some trouble. Just a few days before Freddie drowned, Clayton remembered Glenn saying that Andrew seemed to be baiting Freddie and Glenn had told him to knock it off."

"It doesn't seem like enough of a motive to kill someone," I said. "Would Andrew have been kicked out of the program for letting a couple of people turn in an assignment a bit late? That seems a little harsh."

"I agree," Mr. P. said, "but it's something worth looking into."

"If Freddie was very much about following the rules, maybe she had managed to antagonize someone else, maybe one of the students in her group," Mac suggested.

Mr. P. nodded and pushed his glasses up his nose. "Something else worth looking into."

"That's really all Clayton could tell me," Charlotte said.

"It's a start," Rose said. "Thank you."

Charlotte went to put her apron on and Mac said

he'd be out in the garage workshop for a few minutes before he took Rose and Mr. P. to their meetings. Rose went upstairs to "add a little hot to the teapot," as she put it.

Mr. P. and I were left alone in the office. "I need your opinion on something," I said.

"What's on your mind, my dear?" he said.

I set my coffee mug on the table. "I keep thinking about what Michelle said about drawing my own conclusions. Maybe I'm trying to read too much into her words, but I can't shake the feeling it was some kind of message. On the other hand, I could be trying to turn a random comment into something important. And either way, I just don't seem to be able to let the pieces fall into place."

"It was wrong of me to tell you to do that," he said. "I was dismissive of your concerns. Would you mind sharing exactly what Michelle said to you? Maybe we can figure something out."

I nodded. "She said I saw the body and I said yes. Then she said I was on that stretch of sand and I said yes again. That's when she said maybe I should draw my own conclusions. Maybe what I should be doing is not trying to make her words into some kind of secret message."

"I'm sure you've heard the expression 'Sometimes a cigar is just a cigar,'" Mr. P. said.

I smiled. "Sigmund Freud."

He nodded. "While the phrase is attributed to Freud, there is actually no evidence that he ever said it, but I do agree with the sentiment, no matter where it originated. In this case maybe a comment was just an idle comment, or maybe Michelle was trying to lead you in a certain direction. Whichever is the case, how could it hurt to think about what you saw? Maybe you'll learn something, and if you don't, then no harm has been done." He narrowed his gaze. "Have I been helpful at all?"

Somehow his reasoned response helped. "You have," I said with a smile. "Thank you."

I went back to the shop, where Charlotte was trying two bright red seat cushions she'd brought from home on the bench. "Oh, I like the way they look," I said. "They make the bench look like somewhere I'd actually want to sit down."

"They're from that long wooden seat I used to have on the back patio that no one ever sat on."

I grinned. "That's because it was the most uncomfortable piece of furniture ever made and no cushions were going to fix that."

Charlotte put one hand on her hip and gave me a look. "Maybe you've forgotten that wooden bench came from this store."

"Doesn't change a thing," I said.

She smiled. "I also brought a couple of blue and red pillows to tuck at each end of the seat." She pulled them out of her canvas tote bag. "There," she said, setting each pillow in place. "All we need now is the right person to come in and see this."

Mac left about half an hour later to take Mr. P. and Rose to their meetings. "I need to stop for a couple of things at the hardware store," he said.

"Take your time," I said, gesturing to the empty store. "It's not exactly busy here."

Since we had no customers, Charlotte and I spent some time looking through a box of old framed photos of North Harbor that Avery had found when she organized the under-the-stairs storage space.

"I'm embarrassed to admit it, but I forgot all about them," I said to Charlotte. We picked half a dozen of the photos to hang and spread them out on an old sheet on the floor, trying to settle on an arrangement.

I felt my phone vibrate in my pocket. I took it out and checked the screen. It was Jess. "Maybe she has some new pillows for us," I said.

"We could put a couple of them on that bench," Charlotte said.

"Hey, Jess," I said. "What's going on?"

"Are you really busy?" she asked.

"No more than usual. What do you need?"

Jess cleared her throat and then lowered her voice. "Joanna Norris is here." "Here" had to mean in her shop. "She wants to talk to you."

"Rose and Mr. P. aren't there right now," I said.

"They don't need to be. The person Joanna wants to talk to is you."

Chapter 12

For a moment I wasn't sure I'd heard Jess correctly. "Me?" I said. "Joanna Norris wants to talk to me? Why?"

"I'm not sure," Jess said. "She came into the store a few minutes ago. She asked if you and I are friends and I said yes, we've been friends for a long time. Then she asked me if I would connect the two of you. She wants to talk to you. I think it might be because you found her brother's body."

"Actually it was Cleveland who found the body. "

"I know that." Jess said, "but somehow I think Joanna would feel better talking to you, no offense to Cleveland. Could you make some time for her? Please, Sarah?"

I nodded, even though Jess couldn't see me. "If it works, come right now. It's pretty quiet this morning."

"Thanks," she said. "Right now works for me. I'll see you in a few minutes."

We ended the call and I put my phone back in my

pocket. I turned to Charlotte, who had gone back to arranging the photos. "You're not going to believe this," I said. "That was Jess. Joanna Norris wants to talk to me, probably because I was there when Cleveland found her brother's body." I swallowed a couple of times. I wasn't looking forward to this.

"The poor child," Charlotte said, standing up and brushing off the front of her apron. "Joanna was in one of my English classes. Very quiet but very smart. You know, her brother was the only family she had. Their parents died years ago and as far as I know there are no aunts and uncles, no cousins."

I wrapped Charlotte in a hug.

She looked a little surprised. "Goodness! What was that for? Not that it wasn't very nice."

"I'm just glad you're here," I said. "I'm so lucky to have so many people around me—you and Rose and Liz and Mr. P. and Avery and Nick—you're all like family—you are family. I don't know what I'd do without all of you. I don't know what I'd do if I were in Joanna Norris's place."

Charlotte patted my cheek. "You are never going to find out," she said, "because we are always going to be your family and for the record, as far as everyone is concerned, we are a perfectly nice, normal family."

I laughed. "I don't think anyone thinks we're normal," I said.

We played around with the photos for a few more minutes and finally decided on a layout that both of us were happy with. Charlotte took a photo of the photos before we picked them up off the floor. We finished just as Jess and Joanna walked in.

Joanna Norris was tiny, no more than five feet tall. She had pale blue eyes, fair hair pulled back in a loose braid and long side bangs. She was wearing black yoga pants, a white V-neck T-shirt and an embellished jean jacket that I recognized as being one of Jess's creations.

Jess introduced us and Joanna gave me a tentative smile. "Thank you for talking to me," she said.

"I hope I can help," I said.

Joanna looked at Charlotte and frowned. "Mrs. Elliot?" she said.

Charlotte smiled and took Joanna's hands in hers, giving them a gentle squeeze. "It's good to see you, Joanna," she said. "I was so sorry to hear about Michael."

"Thank you," Joanna said. "What are you doing here?"

Charlotte smiled. "I work here part-time."

Joanna looked at Jess and me. "Mrs. Elliot was one of my favorite teachers. I had always thought poetry and Shakespeare were boring, but they weren't in her class."

I smiled. "Charlotte was a lot of people's favorite teacher." I gestured at the stairs. "Why don't we go up to my office?"

"Would it be all right if Jess comes, too?" she asked.

"Of course," I said. I looked at Charlotte. "Mac will be back soon."

Charlotte looked around the shop. "I think I can handle this," she said.

Joanna smiled at her. "I'm glad I got to see you," she said.

"I'm glad I got to see you as well," Charlotte said.

We went upstairs and settled in my office. I offered coffee or tea but Joanna turned down both. "So why did you want to talk to me?" I asked.

She hesitated. "I know you . . . you were there when my brother's . . . my brother's body was found."

"I was," I said. "I'm so sorry."

"So you . . . saw him?" Her hands were on her lap and she was picking at the skin on her left thumb with the middle finger of her other hand.

I nodded.

"Did he . . . did he look like he suffered?"

Jess pressed her lips together but didn't say anything.

I flashed back to the seaweed and piece of blue tarp wrapped around Michael Norris's head. I took a breath and let it out slowly before I answered, choosing my words with care. "I didn't really see his face," I said. "He was . . . just floating. He looked . . . quiet."

"Thank you," Joanna said. "Knowing that helps." She continued to pick at her thumb. "The police think that Michael may have eaten something he was allergic to—he had an allergy to sesame seeds. I'm a nurse and I know what anaphylaxis is like. I hate to think of my big brother struggling to get his last few breaths."

"I give you my word that from what I could see, he didn't look like that at all," I said. And I thought that if he had, I wasn't sure I would have told Joanna the truth.

"What I don't understand is what Michael was doing out on that stretch of beach. I'm sure you know what happened out there."

"I do," I said.

Jess nodded.

"It's been almost fifteen years since Freddie died and the police seem to think that was why Michael was out there, but it doesn't make sense to me. He would never have done something like that. According to them he had a water bottle, some soft pretzels and a container of hummus like he was planning on being there for a while."

I leaned forward in my chair. "Joanna, why did your brother eat hummus if he was allergic to sesame seeds? Tahini is part of the flavor."

"I don't know how much you know about food allergies," she said, "but you can develop a food allergy later in life, even to something you used to be able to eat. Michael didn't become allergic to sesame seeds until he was in his teens. He had always been a picky eater and hummus was the way our mom got him to eat at least some vegetables. When his allergy was discovered Mom started making hummus for him with sunflower butter instead of the tahini. I make"— she stopped and corrected herself—"made it for him fairly often."

The door opened and Elvis padded in. He made his way over to Joanna, looked up at her and meowed. She smiled down at him. "Is this your cat?" she asked.

I nodded. "Yes, this is Elvis."

"Is he friendly?"

Jess laughed. "Oh yeah."

"Too friendly sometimes," I said.

I barely had the words out and Elvis jumped onto her lap.

I shook my head. "I'm sorry. As you can see, he doesn't always have very good manners."

Joanna was already smiling and stroking the cat's fur. "You're so handsome," she said. She studied his face and then gestured at his nose. "How did he get that scar?"

"I don't know," I said. "It's part of his past life, or maybe lives, for all I know. He has some other scars under his fur and the vet says he was most likely in a fight at some point."

Elvis held out a paw to Jess, who reached over and gave him a little scratch under his chin.

"Elvis was hanging around downtown and thanks to a friend he ended up coming to live with me," I said. "No one knows where he came from."

"Why did you name him Elvis?" Joanna asked.

"Because he's just not a Stones fan," Jess said with a shrug.

"Me neither," Joanna whispered and Elvis seemed to smile at her words.

She looked across the desk at me, continuing to stroke Elvis's fur. "I know that you and your friends have helped solve several crimes in the past, and that you're helping Glenn now. I've known Glenn since I was a kid—he and Michael had been friends since middle school—and I give you my word that Glenn wouldn't have killed my brother. Their friendship may have ebbed and flowed, but in the end, they were very loyal to each other."

I nodded. It seemed clear that Joanna didn't know Glenn had found out Michael was hiding information about Freddie Black's murder.

"According to the police, Michael and Glenn argued on the day he died. I'm afraid they think that Glenn convinced Michael to meet him out where he died. I admit that Glenn is pretty much the only person who would be able to have gotten my brother out there. They found hummus in Michael's refrigerator, which makes sense because I had made some for him on the weekend. There was part of a package of soft pretzels as well. Of course there was no tahini in the hummus from the fridge, but the jar in his backpack had both sunflower butter and tahini."

Jess and I exchanged a look.

"I'm convinced that someone was trying to provoke an allergic reaction in Michael, but it wasn't Glenn. He just wouldn't do that."

Elvis was still happily purring on her lap.

"Do you have any idea who might have wanted to hurt your brother?" I asked.

She nodded. "Yes. Whoever really killed Freddie Black."

Chapter 13

I stared at her in shock. "I'm sorry," I finally managed to say. "I don't understand."

From the contented look on Elvis's face, which hadn't changed the entire time he had been sitting peacefully on Joanna's lap, he believed what she had just said.

"You know that Andrew Lewis went to prison for killing Freddie," Joanna said.

"I know that," I said. "He took a plea."

"An Alford plea. Andrew has always maintained he's innocent. He didn't kill Freddie."

"There were two witnesses who saw Andrew and Freddie arguing out on the breakwater, and the police found Andrew's St. Christopher medal where they had been standing."

She nodded. "You're right about that." She pushed her bangs back from her face with one hand. "I used to hang around my brother and his friends a lot. I was the annoying little sister. There are—there were—almost four years between Michael and me and he was a year younger than his friends because he skipped a year in school."

She smiled. "He didn't always want me around but that didn't stop me. I can tell you that Freddie and Andrew were always bickering about something. They disagreed about everything, from music to food to what books they were reading to Einstein's unified theory." She shook her head. "That's just what their relationship was like."

I glanced at Elvis. His expression hadn't changed.

"And as far as that St. Christopher medal," she went on, "it had a loose catch. I found it on the back-seat of Michael's car twice. Andrew said he probably lost it when he was swimming and it just happened to wash up on the breakwater."

"You think Andrew Lewis is innocent," I said.

"I don't think it. I know it," she said. "The evidence was circumstantial. The so-called witnesses had only seen Andrew and Freddie arguing and they were al-ways doing that. Anyone who knew them well knew that. And those witnesses had both been drinking."

She held up one finger. "As for the bruises on Fred-die's body, there's more than one way they could have been caused."

"So why did Andrew take the Alford plea?" I asked.

Anger flashed in her pale blue eyes. "Because the lawyer his parents hired for him advised him to do that. He said if Andrew didn't, he could end up in jail for the rest of his life."

"So who do you think killed Freddie?" Jess asked. Aside from the comment about Elvis it was the first time she'd spoken.

Joanna shifted in her seat to look at Jess.

"Freddie was teaching a tutorial section for a first-year statistics class. I heard her and Andrew arguing about the fact that she had failed a couple of students." Joanna turned her attention back to me again. "I'm not saying that's a reason for someone to kill her, but Freddie's murder didn't seem to be premeditated. If one of those students had found out about the party from someone and came to confront Freddie, a combination of anger and alcohol could have resulted in them lashing out."

There was a mechanical pencil on my desk and I rolled it across the desktop from one hand to the other. "Were you at the party?" I asked.

She shrugged. "Like I said, I was the pain in the backside little sister. I wasn't invited."

I smiled. "But you were there."

Joanna ducked her head for a moment, then looked me in the eye again. "Yes," she said. "I was there. I just hung around and tried to stay out of Michael's way because he would have pitched a fit if he'd known I was there, and out of Glenn's way because he would have ratted me out to Michael. I talked to a couple of cute guys, drank half a beer and then left because I was afraid Michael would catch on to me being there. It was harder to stay out of his way than I expected, and the half a beer made me feel sick."

She'd stopped scratching behind Elvis's ear and he butted her hand to get her attention again.

"Did you know any of the other people at the party?" I asked.

"Some of them," she said. "Like I said, there weren't

that many people, I'm guessing maybe a dozen or so."

"Could you make me a list of all the names you can remember?"

Joanna nodded. "I didn't know everyone, but I could probably come up with some of the names." She smiled down at Elvis. "I talked to Glenn. He told me what Michael told him about seeing someone else with Freddie. I know that he told you as well."

"Yes, he did," I said. Out of the corner of my eye I saw Jess frown.

"I didn't want to believe it at first, but Michael had started acting different in the past couple of weeks."

"Different how?" I asked.

"He wasn't sleeping well and he wouldn't go the doctor, although I tried to talk him into it. He looked to me like he'd lost weight. And then there was his drinking."

"So he was drinking a lot more?" Jess asked. She had turned sideways, one arm across the back of her chair.

"Just the opposite," Joanna said. "He stopped altogether. Now I think I understand why. According to the police Michael might have seen something the night Freddie died and not told anyone. He just couldn't live with what he'd done any longer."

I remembered what Glenn had said about Andrew Lewis's grandmother having died recently. I could see how that might make it hard for Michael to live with what he'd done. As Rose would say, guilt is a powerful motivator.

"I know that it might not be possible to find out who killed my brother, but please, don't let Glenn be blamed for it. Don't let one mistake in judgment on Michael's part turn into two. Don't let him mess up someone else's life. Please."

Her voice was edged with emotion and her hands were clenched into tight fists. "I'm ashamed of Michael for keeping quiet about what he saw, and I'm not sure the information will help Andrew now, but I will do anything to fix things. He's the most important person in the world to me!" She closed her eyes for a moment. "I'm sorry," she said softly.

I held up one hand. "It's okay," I said. "I have a brother. I'd do anything for him. I get it. We'll do our very best to help Glenn and figure out who killed Michael."

Joanna took a deep breath and let it out. "Thank you," she said. She smiled at Elvis again. "I'm so glad I got to meet you." She set him on the floor. We headed back downstairs.

Charlotte was marking little X's on the wall, presumably for the photos. Joanna excused herself and went to speak to her. Jess and I stayed at the bottom of the stairs. She shook her head. "The best word to describe how I feel is gobsmacked."

"That sounds like the right word to me," I said. "You get that I need you to keep everything you heard to yourself?"

"You have my word," she said, making a little X over her heart with one finger.

"And thank you for bringing Joanna here."

She smiled. "Hey, I like Glenn. I'm glad I could help."

Joanna hugged Charlotte and rejoined us. She thanked me again and promised she'd get the list of names to me as soon as she could. Then she and Jess left.

I raked a hand back through my hair and walked over to Charlotte. "How did the conversation go?" she asked.

"According to Joanna, at this point the police seem to think someone who knew about Michael Norris's allergy tried to use it to kill him."

"We did think that was possible."

"She also believes that Andrew Lewis did not kill Freddie Black."

"Really?" One eyebrow went up.

"And she thinks whoever did kill Freddie also killed her brother."

"Did Joanna offer any idea as to who this person is?" Charlotte asked.

"She did not," I said. "She did mention some conflicts Freddie had with a couple of students in the tutorial class she taught, but that was it."

Before I could say anything else, two women came in. I recognized one of them as the owner of a small inn located in Camden, close to their harbor front. She was looking for a couple of chairs and a set of dishes with a dozen place settings.

"We have two sets of dishes that will serve twelve," Charlotte said. "I'll go get a plate from each set."

"What kind of chairs are you looking for?" I asked, trying to figure out which ones to bring out to show her.

She gave me a wry smile. "I don't really know," she

said. "I need two more places to sit in our front parlor and I need something easy to move. I'm not looking for anything very big, either."

I smiled at her. "I have a couple of ideas," I said. "Give me a minute."

Charlotte came back with the plates so I went out to the workroom. I brought out a wooden farmhouse chair that I estimated was over a hundred years old, painted a warm blue-green color with wide-spaced legs and a rope seat. Then on impulse I also brought one of two chairs we had on consignment from the last house we had cleared out. It was an antique Dutch corner knitting chair with hand-turned bobble legs and rush seats dating from the early 1900s. Both of the chairs were a lot more expensive than what I usually offered, but both had caught my eye and I knew they'd catch someone else's as well.

The two women were immediately taken with the corner chair. "And you have the second one?" the inn owner asked.

I nodded. "Yes, I do," I said, "and I should warn you the chairs are expensive, over six hundred dollars for the pair."

"I'll take them," she said without hesitation.

I felt a sudden urge to do a little touchdown dance, but managed to restrain myself.

She turned her attention to the plates Charlotte had set on a small, round end table. Her friend walked over to the photos we were getting ready to hang. I joined her and pointed out various North Harbor landmarks.

"When were these taken?" she asked.

"As far as we can tell, sometime in the early 1960s," I said. "Unfortunately there's nothing to identify the photographer."

In the end we sold the two corner chairs, a set of Dimity Rose china, the round table Charlotte had set the plates on and three of the photos. I wrapped the chairs and table in some old thrift store blankets I kept just for that. Charlotte took care of packing the dishes.

As the two women drove away, Mr. P. came along the sidewalk. I waited for him, glad to be outside in the sunshine. "How did coffee with Merton go?" I asked.

He smiled. "I think it went quite well, although I do need to educate Merton's palate with respect to his coffee choices."

"You did it with all of us," I said. "I'm certain you can enlighten Merton."

"Thank you for the vote of confidence," he said as we made our way toward the back. "In your case you already recognized an excellent bean when you tasted it."

I gave him a gentle bump with my shoulder. "But I wasn't above drinking lukewarm vending machine coffee, either."

He held up a finger. "I believe we agreed that was something we were no longer going to talk about. So I'm going to change the subject. How was your morning?"

I smiled. "I sold those two corner chairs from Homer Dixon's house."

"I am impressed," he said.

"That's not all. Joanna Norris was here."

He gave me an approving smile. "It seems both our mornings have been productive so far."

We headed into the shop where Charlotte had gotten three more framed photos from under the stairs to replace the three we had just sold. One of them was of the old sail factory back in its heyday where the new vegan restaurant was located today. Mr. P. knew a little about each location in the photos.

"Would you write up a brief paragraph to hang beside each photograph?" I asked. "I think customers would be even more interested if they knew a bit about what they're looking at. Especially younger customers."

"I'd be happy to," Mr. P. said.

Charlotte nodded. "That's a wonderful idea. Even I don't recognize some of these places and I don't exactly fit in the younger category."

"You're not old," I said. "You're young at heart."

Charlotte laughed. "Tell that to my knees in the morning."

I gathered the photos and carried them down to the Angels' office. "There's no rush on this," I told Mr. P.

"I'm looking forward to it," he said. "Now tell me how Joanna Norris ended up here."

I explained about Jess calling. "I would rather you and Rose had been here, but I didn't want to lose this chance to talk to her."

"Oh, you absolutely did the right thing," he said.

"Joanna doesn't believe Andrew Lewis killed Freddie and she thinks whoever did kill her also killed

Michael. Presumably because this person, whoever they are, found out that Michael may have seen them."

"Did Joanna offer any suggestions as to who this person is?"

"One of a couple of nameless, faceless students that Freddie apparently failed in her tutorial section. It feels like a bit of a stretch to me."

"To me as well," he said. "But I also think it is an idea that's worth looking into. It shouldn't be that hard to find those two people. There will be class records to look at. Let me poke around a little."

I brushed a bit of cat hair off my pants. "What did you learn from Merton?" I asked.

"As far as the neighbors were concerned Michael Norris was a bit of a prickly person, according to Merton. And there were other people who had issues with him as well. One person I think we need to look into is a man named Tyrell Warren, a former tenant in one of two apartment buildings Michael owned. Apparently they had a very loud and heated argument and Mr. Warren threatened to remove Michael Norris's head from his body, hollow it out and use it for a dip bowl. Mr. Norris had evicted Tyrell because of ongoing noise complaints."

"A dip bowl," I said. "Tyrell Warren sounds like a very . . . dramatic person."

"He certainly does," Mr. P. agreed. "I'll see what I can find out about him as well."

I heard a noise behind us and turned around to see Rose and Mac coming in the back door. Mac was carrying two cans of paint. Rose smiled when she noticed us.

"I'm just going to put this paint on the workbench and I'll be right back," Mac said.

"How did you make out?" I asked Rose.

"It was a productive meeting," she said. "Josh is a fine young man, no surprise given that Jane is his mother."

Jane Evans was Liz's assistant. She was calm and even and, as Mr. P. explained it, kept Liz's professional life running like a Swiss train schedule.

"I'm not at all surprised he became a lawyer," I said, sitting on the corner of Mr. P.'s desk. "Josh argued us all out of trouble more than once when he was a kid. Gram said it was easier to give in because Josh did not quit. He was so reasoned and so logical in his black-framed glasses with tape on one corner and his purple Darkwing Duck cape."

Rose smiled. "And he was so polite and well-mannered." She took off her sweater. "For this case we are now working for Josh, not Glenn."

"I'm pleased to hear that," Mr. P. said. "That gives Glenn a little more protection."

Rose patted her hair. "He said if there's anything we think Michelle should know, he'll take care of that." She looked at Mr. P. and me in turn. "Have you two come up with anything?"

"Mr. P. has a possible suspect, thanks to his conversation with Merton," I said. "And I have a couple of vaguer suspects, thanks to Jess showing up with Joanna Norris. You were right. The police do seem to think Michael Norris was murdered and that someone used his allergy against him."

Rose beamed. "I knew it," she said.

I leaned sideways and kissed her cheek. "It's annoying how often you're right."

"Not to me, it isn't," she said.

"I need to get back to the shop but Mr. P. will bring you up to date on everything."

Behind her, Liz said, "Don't move a muscle, missy. I have something to tell you all and I don't want to have to say it twice."

"We're listening," Rose said. "What is it?"

I turned to look at Liz.

"Andrew Lewis, the young man who went to prison for the murder that happened on that beach fifteen years ago, might be the person who killed Michael Norris."

"That's not possible, Elizabeth," Mr. P. said. "He's in prison."

Liz shook her head. "No, he's not."

Chapter 14

Rose stared at Liz for a long moment. "What do you mean, he's not in prison?"

"I mean exactly what I said," Liz said, making a sweeping gesture with one hand. "Andrew Lewis is no longer in prison."

"How could that have happened?" I asked. I glanced at Mr. P., who looked as surprised as I felt.

"He was released early. Overcrowding."

"When?" Mr. P. asked.

"About two weeks ago," Liz said.

"How do you know this?" Rose asked.

Liz shrugged. "I pay attention and I may have stirred the pot a little."

Rose's gaze narrowed. "And what exactly do you mean by 'stirred the pot a little'?"

I was wondering the same thing. Liz didn't do things "a little." She fell more into the category of "go big or stay home."

"I went for a manicure and really didn't find out a

damn thing, but when I finally got the conversation around to Michael Norris it turned very easily to the death of Freddie Black and I learned from another customer that Layla Cunningham, who does some kind of fancy foot treatment with seaweed, is related somehow to Freddie. So of course I had to go talk to Ms. Cunningham about her treatment and while we were talking she mentioned that her cousin's killer is out of jail and she wouldn't be surprised if he had something to do with Michael Norris's murder."

I wondered how Liz had managed to steer the conversation from a seaweed foot treatment to Andrew Lewis getting out of prison, but if anyone could do that, she could. She handed me a pale lavender envelope.

"What's this?" I asked, even though I had an idea.

"It's a gift certificate for the full foot saver package for your knobby feet. The appointment is for three weeks from Monday."

"Thank you," I said, putting the envelope in my pocket.

"Elizabeth, do you know where Andrew Lewis is staying?" Mr. P. asked.

Liz shook her head. "I don't, but I can get Jane to find out." Josh's mother was almost as good as Mr. P. at ferreting out information.

"Thank you," he said, "but I can do that."

Rose smiled at Liz. "Thank you. You may have just given us our best suspect so far."

"I like Glenn," Liz said, "and I don't want to see him blamed for something any rationally thinking person would know he didn't do."

That felt like a dig at Michelle but I decided to let it pass.

Liz looked at her watch. "I have somewhere I need to be," she said.

I took her by the arm. "I'll walk you out." I looked down at the sleek black slingbacks she was wearing. "Maybe I could borrow a pair of your shoes once my feet are all beautiful."

Liz gave a snort of laughter. "First of all, the young woman is an aesthetician, not a plastic surgeon, and second of all, there's no way your feet would fit in my shoes. They would stretch them all out of shape, no offense."

I laughed. "None taken. Everyone knows you have the feet of a ten-year-old."

"And everyone knows you have the feet of a lumberjack," Liz retorted.

I pressed my cheek to hers for a moment. "Thank you, you spoil me."

Liz smiled. "Go do something useful. I have places to go and people to see." She blew me a kiss and she was gone.

I turned around and saw Mac standing by the workbench, talking on his phone and smiling about something. I walked over to join him as he ended the call.

"Jameis is finally coming for a visit," he said. "No last-minute cancelation. He promised."

"When?" I asked. We'd been trying to organize a visit for what felt like forever.

"The end of the week sometime. He's flying standby so he's not positive what day he'll get here. He's flying into Portland and I'll drive down and pick him up."

I grinned at Mac. "I'm so happy this visit is finally happening."

Mac nodded. "Me too. It's been way too long."

Jameis was a travel nurse who had been working most recently in Alaska. He and I had gotten to be friends via video calls, but I was happy we were finally going to meet in person.

"You know Charlotte is going to want to have a family dinner. It might be a little overwhelming."

"Not for Jameis," Mac said. "He's an extrovert. He'll know three quarters of North Harbor by his second day here."

"I need to ask Rose one more thing, but first I want to see what paint you chose."

He gave me a sheepish look. "I couldn't exactly narrow it down to one color, so I bought two. I was hoping for your opinion."

I put a hand on my chest. "I am full of opinions," I said.

Mac laughed. "You're full of something." He opened both cans. One was a medium brown the color of chocolate mousse and the other a vivid cardinal red.

"Is this for the old dresser you're turning into a kitchen island?" I asked.

"Yes," he said.

"The red then."

He looked surprised.

"The red will stand out, and while I wouldn't want all-red cabinets in my kitchen, I'd love a red island if I actually had room for an island at all."

"Red it is then," Mac said.

"I do like the brown," I said. "We'll find a use for it."

I went back to the office. Rose was on her phone, standing by the windows overlooking the parking lot.

"She's talking to Josh's assistant about helping us find Andrew Lewis," Mr. P. said.

"I got sidetracked," I said, "and I didn't ask Rose what's next."

"Are you up for a small road trip at the end of the day?"

"Who are we going to ambush?" I asked.

"'Ambush' is a rather loaded word," he said, a hint of a smile playing across his face.

"Okay," I said. "How about ensnare, waylay, bushwhack?"

His smile got bigger. "I'd like to pay a visit to Tyrell Warren."

"The tenant Michael Norris evicted."

Mr. P. nodded. "It's somewhere to start while we try to locate Andrew Lewis and see if we can track down the two students Freddie Black failed."

"That works for me," I said.

He smiled. "Splendid. And for what it's worth I don't think you have lumberjack feet."

Charlotte was showing a customer an old wooden ironing board in the shop. She beckoned me over to the cash desk.

Her customer introduced himself as Jon Everly. He was about average height with a smoothly shaven head and blue-framed glasses. "My mother is friends with Stella Hall," he said. "Stella recommended you as someone to clear out a house. She said you took care of her late brother's home."

"We did," I said. I didn't say that it got us tied up in a murder, since there had been a body in the kitchen.

"Could you give me a general idea of what you do?" he asked. "My mother's sister has gone into assisted living and we're both overwhelmed by everything that needs to be done."

"Would you like to come up to my office?" I asked. "Or I could email you with the details."

"I'll come up to your office," he said. "Thank you."

I spent about ten minutes explaining what we did when we cleared out someone's home, everything from emptying the house of furniture to packing personal items to selling things on consignment in the shop. Mr. Everly told me a little about his aunt's home, which was a large two-story house from the mid-nineteenth century, and we agreed that I would take a look at the house on Wednesday morning.

Mr. Everly collected his ironing board and I rejoined Charlotte to find Avery had arrived. I knew she'd had an exam that morning, which was probably why she was early. I asked how it went. Avery made a face. I let her be and walked over to Charlotte, who was adding a teddy bear to the child's rocking horse in the window.

She smiled. "Is Mr. Everly going to hire us?"

"I think so," I said. I told her about the planned visit to check out the house tomorrow. "Would you be able to come in for the whole day? I'd like to take Mac with me to the meeting."

"I'd be happy to," she said.

The afternoon was busy. Joanna sent me the list of people she remembered from the party. There were five names on it. Mr. P. told me he had asked for the same kind of list from Glenn.

"When I receive it I'll compare the two and see if I can eliminate anyone. Glenn is the one who organized the party and he said he invited half a dozen people. As far as he remembers, Freddie and Andrew each invited one other person. He said he doesn't remember seeing anyone he didn't know but it was almost fifteen years ago and memories get hazy in that amount of time."

"Even a few names are better than none," I said.

"I've also started trying to track down the two students Freddie failed in her tutorial," he said.

"And do I want to know how you're doing that?" I asked.

"I'm very charming," he said with a smile.

I laughed. "That you are, Mr. P."

At the end of the day Mac took Charlotte and Avery with him. He was going to look at a boat trailer. Avery was having supper with Charlotte and then she and Greg were heading to the library to study, but before that Greg was going to carry up some boxes from Charlotte's basement that she wanted to look through. In return he got to take home a very large aquarium that had once belonged to Nick. "And I can't say I'm going to miss that monstrosity," Charlotte confided.

Rose, Mr. P. and Elvis came with me. Elvis settled himself on the backseat next to Mr. P. Sometimes the cat chose to sit back there and other times he sat up front next to Rose. In either spot he was very much a backseat driver.

I fastened my seat belt and started the SUV. "Where are we headed?" I asked.

"Do you know where Windward Way is?" Mr. P. asked.

"I do," I said. "It's a short dead end street that climbs uphill from the harbor."

"We're looking for number nineteen," Rose said.

"Did you have any luck finding out where Andrew Lewis is living?" I asked her.

"Yes, as a matter of fact, I did. He's staying at a halfway house. It's not going to be easy to talk to him there."

"So what's the plan then?"

I saw Rose cast a brief glance over her shoulder. "I'm still working out the details," she said. She straightened up in her seat and folded her hands in her lap.

I wondered if she and Alfred were having a disagreement about their next step and I decided not to ask any more questions.

We turned onto Windward Way. "Could you keep an eye on the street numbers, please?" I said to Rose. The street was narrow and steep. There was enough space for two vehicles to just pass, but no more.

"They start at one," she said, "so nineteen must be higher up the hill."

Number nineteen Windward Way turned out to be the last house on the right-hand side at the end of the street. The house was set back from the curb, surrounded by tall trees that provided a fair amount of privacy. I parked in front and we got out. Elvis jumped onto the front seat and made himself comfortable in the middle.

The house was a small, one-story cottage from about the 1920s, I guessed. It was painted white with a bright yellow front door. Mr. P. knocked and after a moment the door was answered by a large African American man, wearing jeans and a purple dashiki with detailed gold embroidery. He was easily six foot four or five, heavyset with striking blue eyes. The fact that he was wearing long false eyelashes and a warm smile made him look far less imposing than he probably otherwise would have.

By unspoken agreement Rose took the lead. She answered the man's smile with a warm one of her own. "Are you Tyrell Warren?" she asked.

"Yes, I am," he said.

"I'm Rose Jackson," she said. "This is Alfred Peterson and Sarah Grayson. Alfred and I are private investigators looking into the death of Michael Norris."

His smile disappeared. "That was absolutely tragic," he said. "Please, come in."

He led us into a sun-filled living room with a large, comfortable-looking navy blue sofa and two 1970s vintage Danish-style armchairs covered in bright orange fabric. The whole room exploded with color, from the purple batik curtains framing the windows to the multicolored cushions on the sofa to the iridescent candy dish on the low coffee table.

"This room is beautiful," I said, looking around to take it all in.

Tyrell beamed at me. "Thank you," he said. "I

always say, if a little color is good, a lot is better." He invited us to sit down and took one of the two chairs for himself. "How can I help you?"

"You used to live in one of Michael Norris's apartment buildings," Mr. P. said.

He nodded. "Yes, I did." Then recognition spread across his face. "You heard about our argument."

"Yes, we did," Rose said. "After all, you did threaten to turn your landlord's head into a dip bowl."

Tyrell smiled. "I can be a rather dramatic person at times. Certainly everyone in the building *heard* our argument."

"You don't seem at all angry at Mr. Norris, considering he kicked you out of your apartment," Rose said.

The man's blue eyes narrowed. "Wait a minute, you don't think I did anything to Michael because he evicted me, do you? I've heard the speculation that his death might not have been an accident."

"It did cross our minds," Mr. P. said.

"I am a large person in every way, not just size, Mr. Peterson," Tyrell said. "I live life with enthusiasm and I'm not quiet about it. I'm an opera singer and I aspire to be the next Morris Robinson."

"You're a bass as well, I'm guessing," Mr. P. said.

Tyrell nodded. "I am. My neighbors in the building did not appreciate my practice sessions."

He made a dismissive gesture with one hand. "What can I say, they're Philistines. Michael did tell me I had to move, but he also helped me find this house to rent, where I can practice as much as I want to. I was grateful to Michael. I would never have hurt him. And for the record I do have an alibi."

"May I ask what it is?" Mr. P. said.

"I was in Portland having a lesson with my music teacher. I left here right after lunch and I got back about seven. And, most importantly, I suffer from vasovagal syncope, which means I would have passed out from the emotion of the situation, not to mention any blood."

I had no idea what vasovagal syncope was, but both Rose and Mr. P. looked sympathetic so I did the same, hoping fervently I wasn't wasting the expression on something like a foot fungus.

"That must make it difficult to perform," Mr. P. said.

Tyrell nodded. "It does, but I'm determined to overcome it. I was born to be onstage."

He offered the contact information for his voice teacher. Rose thanked him for talking to us.

"Good luck," he said. "Michael wasn't a bad guy and I hope you find out what happened to him."

We got back in the SUV. Elvis decided to stay up front with Rose.

"That man is not a killer," I said.

"No, he certainly isn't," Rose said.

"I'll check with Tyrell's music teacher just to make sure all the T's are crossed and the I's are dotted but I agree with both of you," Mr. P. said.

I sighed. "So strike one," I said.

Mr. P. nodded. "Yes, my dear. Strike one."

Chapter 15

We drove down Windward Way and headed for home. "What's vasovagal syncope?" I asked.

"It causes people to pass out because of a sudden drop in their blood pressure," Rose said.

"The reaction is caused by certain triggers," Mr. P. added, "such as the sight of blood or a needle, standing too long or a very strong emotion, such as fear."

"So something that's a challenge for a performer like Tyrell."

"Exactly," he said.

His phone made a soft chime. Rose turned and looked over her shoulder at him.

"I have a text from Glenn," Mr. P. said. "It's the names of the people from the party. There are six altogether."

"As soon as we get to the house you and I can compare lists," I said.

"You two do realize that this is akin to trying to

teach a cat to tap dance," Rose said. "There could have been any number of people at that party that Glenn and Joanna didn't happen to see. It's a long stretch of beach."

"Number one, cats are very smart, and number two, why would you want to teach a cat to tap dance in the first place?" I said.

In the rearview mirror I could see Mr. P. smiling. Rose just shook her head.

"You obviously think this is a waste of time. Why?" I said.

"Did you ever have a party your parents didn't know about?" she asked. I could see her watching me from the corner of her eye.

"No," I said carefully.

Rose turned around once more to look at Mr. P. Whatever her former annoyance with him had been about it seemed to be gone now. "Did you see it?" she said.

"Yes, I did," he replied. "You're right."

"Right about what?" I asked.

"I've told you before, you have a tell when you lie," Rose said, her voice matter-of-fact. She *had* told me that before.

"I do not have any tell," I said, a little more vehemently than I had intended. "And anyway, I wasn't lying."

Rose reached over and patted my arm. "Of course you weren't," she said in a tone of voice that indicated she knew I really was. "My point is that people bring other people to parties who weren't invited all the time. So even if we end up with a complete list of everyone who Glenn and Joanna remember seeing, that doesn't mean we have a list of every person who was actually there."

Beside her, Elvis murped his agreement and Rose smiled down at him.

I let out a small sigh of exasperation. "Fine. I'll concede that. But if we talk to everyone on the list, we might be able to find out who, if anyone, was there uninvited."

"She has a point, Rosie," Mr. P. said.

"Yes, she does," Rose agreed, a little grudgingly it seemed to me.

"I had good teachers," I said with a smile.

Rose gave her head a shake. "You're lucky blatant flattery works on me."

When they got to the house I took out my phone and pulled up the list Joanna Norris had sent to me. We stood in the hallway comparing names. Rose picked up Elvis and he craned his neck to look at the phone screens.

"We know we're looking for a minimum of eight names," I said. I looked at Mr. P. "You said Glenn told you he invited half a dozen people and Freddie and Andrew each invited someone."

He nodded.

Joanna's list of five people contained three men's names and two women's. Glenn's six names was split evenly, three and three. All five people from Joanna's list were also on Glenn's.

I sighed in frustration. "We're still missing at least two people."

Mr. P. put his phone back in his pocket. "But as you

pointed out, if we can find any of these six we may be able to get more names."

I nodded. The idea had sounded more promising when I'd been trying to sell the two of them on it. I took Elvis from Rose. "Have a good night, you two," I said.

Rose smiled. "You as well, sweet girl." They went down the hall to Rose's apartment and I unlocked the door to mine.

I was tired and didn't feel like making supper, so I settled for a bowl of tomato soup and a grilled cheese sandwich—a meal I had eaten more times than I wanted to admit before Rose and Charlotte taught me to cook. And now I had upped my game from those days, making the sandwich with sourdough bread and a mix of mozzarella and pepperjack cheeses, a tip I had gotten from Mr. P. The cheese had come from his favorite vendor at the farmers' market and the bread from Glenn's bakery.

After supper I threw in a load of laundry and washed the kitchen and bathroom floors. I was just settling in to watch *Only Murders in the Building* when Elvis walked through the living room, sat just in front of the door and looked expectantly at it. Approximately thirty seconds later I heard a knock. Elvis looked at me. I had no idea how he seemed to know we were about to have a visitor.

"If you could learn to turn a door knob it would make my life a lot easier," I said as I went to see who it was. He flicked his tail at me.

Rose was at my door. "Am I interrupting anything?" she asked.

"No, come in," I said.

She was wearing an apron and pink fuzzy slippers. I'd seen Mr. P. in both items more than once.

"Alf went home and there's something I need a second opinion on."

"Opinions I have," I said. "Have a seat. What's on your mind?"

Rose sat on the sofa and I perched on one arm. "One of the things both Alfred and I learned from Merton is that Michael Norris had a bit of a prickly relationship with his neighbors," she began.

I nodded. "I remember."

"For instance he didn't like Tippi."

Since Tippi had indirectly helped us solve a case, I had a bit of a soft spot for the gray-and-white seagull but even I preferred to have that soft spot from a distance.

"Not everyone is a bird person," I said. It was the most diplomatic thing I could come up with.

"I understand that," Rose said. "But apparently Michael had been bickering with his neighbors to the left, the Glover sisters."

I frowned. "Why does that name sound familiar?"

"Probably because they have been very generous and consistent donors to the school's hot lunch program." Thanks to my grandmother I'd been involved with that project for years myself.

Elvis came and rubbed against my leg. I bent down and picked him up. Rose reached over and gave him a scratch behind one ear.

"What do you know about the two of them?" I asked.

"Addie and Cherry are in their fifties," Rose said. "They've lived in North Harbor all their lives. They have a couple of small businesses they operate and they also own part of a trucking company that's run by their cousins. They're where Charlotte sends her compost."

Okay, now I was lost. "Charlotte sends her compost to a trucking company?" I said.

Rose frowned. "Of course not. Why would she do that? She's one of Addie and Cherry's customers."

"So the Glover sisters have a compost collection service?"

"I just said that, dear," Rose said. "Try to stay focused. Addie and Cherry pick up organic materials every week from their customers, vermicompost everything and sell the resulting fertilizer." She narrowed her eyes. "You do know what vermicomposting is, don't you?"

"It's a way of composting using worms."

She nodded her approval. "Yes, it is. Addie and Cherry also grow flowers and create and sell wedding bouquets."

"Why would Michael have a problem with any of that?" I asked. "Did he have something against worms? Those women sound like environmentalists."

Elvis murped his agreement.

"Merton told me he didn't know. Michael argued with them multiple times because there were people coming and going at all hours according to him, waking him up and blocking his driveway."

"Hang on," I said. "People were coming and going at all hours to buy flowers and fertilizer?"

Rose nodded. "It seemed odd to me, too."

"Is it possible Michael was exaggerating about the time and the number of cars? Maybe *he* was the difficult neighbor."

"I did think about that," she said, "and maybe that's the case."

"But," I said.

Rose nodded. "Exactly. I just have a feeling."

"I trust your feelings." Experience had taught me Rose's instincts were usually right. All those years of being a teacher had given her a lot of insight into human behavior.

"Alf suggested that perhaps I was looking for trouble where there was none," she said.

"I thought something was a little off between the two of you."

"He's a more logical person and while I do believe in following the facts—" She paused for a moment.

"You also trust your instincts."

Rose nodded. "Yes, I do."

"So what are your instincts telling you in this case?"

"To find out what's going on at the Glover sisters' house."

"So let's do that," I said. I glanced over at the large clock on the wall above the television. "What if we drove over there about eleven o'clock to see what's going on? We're not going to do anything."

"We're just going to wait and see what happens," she said.

Elvis yawned and jumped down to the floor, where he started washing his face.

"Do you think that Addie and Cherry could have

had anything to do with Michael Norris's death?" I asked. "It seems like an extreme way to solve a neighbor problem."

"I don't know," Rose said, "but according to Merton, Michael's allergy to sesame seeds was common knowledge in the neighborhood. He'd been to a couple of community barbeques and he was always very careful about what he ate. If he was a difficult neighbor maybe Addie and Cherry tried to make him sick just to get even."

"That's a dangerous thing to do," I said.

"People do stupid, dangerous things all the time." She was right about that. "Are you sure about our little reconnaissance mission?" she asked.

"If you mean is it stupid and dangerous, no, I don't think it is. We're going to sit in my SUV and watch the house where Addie and Cherry Glover live for maybe half an hour. That's it. We probably won't see anything. So are we going? Eleven o'clock?"

Rose smiled. "Eleven o'clock."

A couple of minutes before eleven p.m., Elvis watched from the top of his cat tower as I zipped up my dark gray hoodie. "If we're not back by one a.m., call the authorities," I told him.

He yawned.

"Assuming you're still awake," I added. I kissed the top of his head and left.

Rose was just coming out of her apartment. Like me she was wearing dark clothes: jeans and a black sweater with a black beanie covering her hair. She was carrying a large thermos.

I looked at her and then down at my own jeans, dark gray T-shirt, hoodie and ball cap. "We look like we're going on a stakeout."

"Aren't we?" she said. "I like to think we're Cagney and Lacey."

I frowned. "Who are they?"

"Only the best female detectives who've ever been on television. And a tiny bit before your time." She waggled a finger at me. "You need to watch a few episodes. You'll thank me."

"Okay," I said, realizing if I didn't, she'd keep after me until I did.

Rose had what looked like a camera case over her shoulder. "Is that a camera?" I asked.

"Binoculars," she said. She held up the thermos. "And hot chocolate."

"Two very good ideas," I said.

Rose raised one eyebrow. "It's not my first rodeo or my first stakeout."

"Not mine, either," I said. "For the record, is hiding in a treehouse and watching Liam sneak out of the house considered a stakeout?"

Rose pretended to think about the question. "I think it meets the criteria," she said after a moment.

"Then I have a fair amount of experience at this kind of thing," I said.

We pulled out of the driveway and headed for Merton's neighborhood, which was soon to be Michelle's new home.

"If the Glovers' house is the one I think it is, we could park on the corner across the street and watch from there," I said.

"We could," Rose said, "or we could park at the bottom of Merton's driveway and watch from there."

I shot her a quick, sideways glance. "And what happens when he notices a strange vehicle in his driveway? I don't want Tippi to attack the car, so to speak."

"I checked with Merton before we left to ask if it would be okay."

"What did you tell him we were going to be doing?" I said.

"I told him the truth, of course," Rose said. As usual she was sitting there with her back straight and her hands folded in her lap. "That we'd be on a stakeout." She gave me a look. "Merton has seen *Cagney and Lacey*."

"He'll tell Mr. P. what we're doing."

"Not necessarily. Merton can be quite circumspect, and it doesn't matter because after you and I find out what's going on, I intend to tell Alf myself."

"So in other words it's easier to get forgiveness than permission—not that we need Mr. P.'s permission to watch a house for half an hour."

"No, we don't," Rose said. She patted my arm. "And you of all people should know about forgiveness versus permission."

Merton's neighborhood was only a few minutes away from my own. His house was in darkness. I backed into the driveway and shut the engine off. The property was one in from the corner.

Rose pointed across the intersection. "The little bungalow on the corner is Michael Norris's house," she said. "The next house in belongs to Addie and Cherry."

I leaned forward for a better look. The Glover house was a small story-and-a-half design, painted medium blue with black shutters and a black front door. It was set back from the street on a large tree-filled lot. There was a single-car garage at the end of the driveway and I could just make out a couple of outbuildings in the fenced backyard. A light was on in the front of the house in what I guessed was the living room. There were no cars parked on the street and no traffic going by.

Rose and I sat in Merton's driveway and watched the Glover house for the next twenty-five minutes. We talked about plans for Avery's graduation party.

"Has Liz said if Avery's mother and father are coming for graduation?" I asked. Avery had a very challenging relationship with her parents, which was why she originally came to live with her grandmother.

"I know that Liz has talked to them and they've been invited, but I don't know if they'll come," Rose said.

"We'll all be there and we're family, too," I said.

At ten minutes to midnight, just as I was about to suggest we call it a night, a half-ton truck came slowly up the street. The driver turned in Michael Norris's driveway and parked in front of his house.

"Well, isn't this interesting," Rose said. She had the binoculars. We had been taking turns using them. "There are two men in the truck."

The streetlight on the corner wasn't working and I leaned over the steering wheel to get a better look. The driver got out and went to the side door of the Glovers' house.

"He's knocking," Rose said.

After a moment I saw the door open and a woman came out.

"That's Addie," Rose said.

The woman was heavyset in jeans with what looked to be a flannel shirt and a baseball cap. She and the man walked back to the truck. Addie lifted up a tarp and looked at something in the bed for a moment. She and the man had a brief conversation, then Addie Glover pulled something out of her pocket.

"What is that in her hand?" I asked Rose.

"Good heavens," Rose exclaimed. "It's a roll of money."

"You can't be serious," I said. Wordlessly Rose handed over the binoculars. I adjusted them and discovered it was a roll of money in Addie's hand, held together, it seemed, by a wide, blue elastic band. It appeared whatever was going on at the Glovers' was a cash business. I knew that wasn't a good sign.

The other man got out of the passenger side of the truck. He was a little shorter than the first man with the same heavyset build. The two men got whatever was in the bed of the truck out, keeping the tarp draped over the top.

"Whatever they're carrying, it looks heavy," I said, handing back the binoculars.

Rose continued to watch as the garage door went up. All three of them disappeared inside and the door came back down again. A couple of minutes later it rose once more and all three came out onto the sidewalk. The men got in their truck and drove away while Addie Glover went back into the house.

Rose leaned back in the seat and looked at me. "Something's definitely going on over there," she said.

I sighed. "You're right, but I don't have a clue what."

"Well, that's what we're going to find out," she said.

Chapter 16

"We agreed we weren't going to do anything stupid or dangerous," I said.

"And I have no intention of doing either of those things," Rose said.

I was already rethinking being here in the first place, because I knew that Rose and I sometimes had different definitions for stupid and dangerous. I thought about the last time the two of us had gone off to check out one of Rose's hunches. We'd gotten out of the situation without either one of us being hurt, but it was a close thing. I still carried some guilt about that and my friendship with Michelle had taken a hit for a time.

"For now, let's just sit here a little longer and see if anyone else shows up. Deal?"

"Deal," Rose said.

In the next half hour we saw the scenario repeated two more times. A vehicle showed up, money changed hands and something was carried into the garage. In one case the driver parked in front of Michael's house again. In the other he parked in front of the neighbor on the other side of the Glover sisters.

"I'm not certain, but I think the house directly across the street from Addie and Cherry may have a doorbell camera and that's why those vehicles aren't parking in front of the house. They don't want to be identified."

"I think you're right," I said. "But what is Addie buying? Whatever it is, it's big and awkward."

"And clearly illegal, given the efforts they're going to avoid being seen."

"I don't see how these transactions can have anything to do with their legitimate businesses," I said, rubbing my stiff left shoulder. "All this activity has to be what Michael was complaining about."

"I'd like to get a closer look at what they're putting in the garage," Rose said.

"So would I," I said, "but we're not getting any closer than we already are."

"We could be looking for your dog."

I glared at her, but the effect was wasted because of the darkness. "I don't have a dog and we're not pretending I do. That falls into the stupid and dangerous category."

When the third transaction took place Rose managed to see that there was a door in the back of the garage. "It looks as though whatever is being carried in is being put in the backyard."

I took the binoculars from her. "I know what you're thinking," I said, "and we're not going to try to sneak into that yard. Given that whatever they're doing is taking place at night, it's a safe bet that the sisters have at least one security camera in that yard."

Rose gave me a look that even in the dark truck was impossible to miss.

"Give me a little credit. I'm not going to try to go into the Glovers' yard. I'm going to go into Michael Norris's yard."

I tilted my head back and stared up at the ceiling of the SUV. "You can't do that, either."

"Why not?"

"Well, for the obvious reason. It's trespassing. If anyone sees you they'll call the police. You could be arrested."

"I'm not going to be arrested. I wouldn't be trespassing. I'd be looking for evidence."

"After midnight on a Tuesday," I said. I felt beside me on the seat for the thermos.

Rose lowered the binoculars. "Yes. If the police show up I'd tell the truth. Michael Norris thought something was going on late at night at his neighbors. We came to try to see what he might have seen. Anyway no one is going to notice me. It's after midnight and everyone is in bed. The Glovers certainly aren't going to call the police."

The thermos was empty. "You drank the last of that about twenty minutes ago," Rose said.

I sighed. "What's your plan? And just because I'm asking doesn't mean I'm going to agree to it."

"See the fence between the two houses?"

"I see it," I said.

"How far would you say that bottom stringer is from the ground?"

"It's hard to say in the dark."

She handed me the binoculars again. I took a look. "Three, maybe four inches," I said, "probably so the wood won't be touching the ground and then rot."

"There's more than enough space to hold a phone underneath and take some photos of what's on the other side."

"It's too dark. The quality of the images will be terrible."

"Not on my phone," Rose said. "I have dark mode. No flash and the quality in low light is very good. I'll just slip over, hold my phone by the gap at the bottom of the fence, take a bunch of photos and come right back. Easy peasy."

I shook my head. "No. The last time we did something like this it almost ended very badly."

"But it didn't. And it won't this time, either."

"I'll take them," I said.

Rose had a stubborn set to her jaw that I knew well. Time to play hardball, as Liz would say. I reached for my seat belt. "Or we can just go home now. Your choice."

For a moment she just sat there. "Fine," she finally said.

She showed me how to use her phone. "If it looks like anything is going wrong, call nine-one-one and stay in the car, please," I said.

Rose pressed her lips together. "Fine," she said again.

I shut off the dome light and got out. I crossed the street, wondering how long the streetlight by Michael's house hadn't been working. I walked up his driveway like I was supposed to be there, thinking that acting like you belong often makes people believe you do belong. At least according to Mr. P.

Luckily the gate into Michael's backyard had a simple latch. I stepped into the yard and immediately dropped into a crouch so no one would see me and I hopefully wouldn't trigger any motion detector lights. Staying low I made my way along two sections of the fence holding the phone up under the gap and taking photo after photo. Mentally I crossed my fingers and hoped this wasn't a waste of time. Finally I put the phone back in my pocket and slipped around the gate, staying close to the house.

Immediately I realized I had a problem. A large SUV was parked in front of the house. I studied it for a moment as I bent down and pretended to tie my shoe. There was no one inside. Maybe I could get out of this.

I walked down the driveway and realized too late there was a man peering into the back of the SUV. He looked at me and I gave an involuntary start. His eyes narrowed. I noticed a sticker in the back window of the vehicle, a dog pawprint with a heart around it.

"Excuse me, have you seen a small, black dog?" I asked. I held out my hand about a foot and a half off the ground. "About this high?"

He shook his head. "Sorry. No."

I exhaled loudly and pushed my bangs away from my face. "I'm staying with a friend and he got out when someone opened the door." I pointed in the general direction of Merton's house.

"What's his name?" the man asked.

"Umm, Fred," I said. "After Mr. Rogers. You know, it's a beautiful day in the neighborhood."

I realized I was babbling and closed my mouth.

"Sorry, can't help you," he said.

I nodded. "Thanks anyway."

I turned toward the intersection and whistled the way I'd heard my friend Ashley Clark whistle for her dog, Casey.

Behind me I heard the man say, ". . . nobody, just some woman looking for a lost dog."

I whistled again, made a show of looking up and down the street and then crossed over to the other side, fighting the impulse to bolt. I whistled a third time just in case they were watching me. As I came level with Merton's driveway I chanced looking back. There was no sign of the man or anyone else.

I ran to the car, jumped in the driver's seat and pulled on my seat belt in one not exactly coordinated motion. I tossed the phone to Rose. "We're getting out of here," I said. I started the SUV and pulled out of Merton's driveway, turning left, away from the Glover sisters' house.

"What happened?" Rose asked. "I saw you talking to someone."

I nodded. "The man who was standing next to that SUV. I said I was looking for my lost dog. Fred." I laughed. "I told him the dog was named after Mr. Rogers."

I glanced over at Rose.

She smiled. "Good thinking on your feet," she said.

I took a long, very roundabout way home. Not that I really believed anyone had followed us, but it didn't hurt to be extra careful.

"How about a cup of tea?" Rose asked when I pulled into the driveway.

I didn't think I was going to be able to sleep anytime soon. I felt as though I was buzzing with adrenaline. "You know, I think I'd like that," I said.

Inside Rose's apartment I took a seat at the table, peeled off my hoodie and ball cap and raked both hands back through my hair. "I can't believe I did that," I said.

"You did well," Rose said, putting a hand on my shoulder for a moment. She sat down at the table and scrolled through all the photos. Many of them were blurry, out of focus or just too dark but several were surprisingly sharp and detailed.

"What's that?" Rose suddenly said. We'd looked at about half the pictures I'd taken, I guessed.

I leaned in to take a closer look at the screen. I'd captured an image of one of the plastic tarps. I realized that one corner of it had slid sideways. "Can you get in a little closer?" I asked Rose.

She expanded the image and I studied it carefully. "It's an exhaust system," I said slowly.

Rose frowned. "Are you sure?"

I nodded.

The kettle began to whistle. Rose got up to make the tea.

I stared off into space trying to pull out the details of a news story I'd heard about a week or so ago. Rose brought over a cup of tea and set a plate with two oatmeal cookies in front of me. I reached for a cookie and the elusive detail came to me.

I looked at Rose. "I know what they're doing." I took a bite of my cookie and smiled.

Rose had a sip of her tea and waited.

"Scroll back three photos, please," I said. I pointed to something sticking out of the edge of the tarp. The quality of the picture overall wasn't good, but it was good enough. "That is a catalytic converter. I saw a story about this on the news. People are stealing them from cars and selling them for the metals inside."

Rose was already nodding. "I saw that story," she said. "Platinum and rhodium are what they're after."

"Addie and Cherry Glover own part of a trucking company. It would be a great way to get these parts out of town to someone who can salvage that metal," I said.

"We need to call the police," Rose said.

I nodded. "But not at this time of night. Nothing is going to happen before the morning." I drank my tea and finished the second cookie. "Do you think Michael knew what was going on next door?"

"It's hard to believe he didn't."

I yawned.

"You need to get some sleep, sweet girl," Rose said.

"You too," I said. I got to my feet and gave her a hug.

"Maybe we've found Michael Norris's killer," she said.

"I hope so," I said, but as I headed to my apartment a small voice in the back of my head whispered, *It just couldn't be this easy.*

Chapter 17

I woke in the morning to Elvis standing on my chest breathing his kitty morning breath in my face. I'd overslept by twenty minutes.

"I'm up," I told him.

He eyed me for a moment and then jumped down to the floor. I sat up and stretched. I didn't function well without enough sleep. Even when I had gotten into bed I couldn't fall asleep right away. My mind was still sorting over what Rose and I had seen and what we had discovered, thanks to the photos.

I stood under the hot water in the shower a little longer than usual, hoping it would wake me up. It didn't.

Elvis meowed indignantly at me when I wasn't fast enough with his breakfast.

"Hey, give me a break," I said. "I was on a stakeout."

He flicked his tail at me. It seemed he didn't think being on a stakeout was a good enough reason for his first meal of the day to be late.

I was staring into the refrigerator, trying to decide what to get for my own breakfast that would require a minimum investment of effort on my part, when I heard a soft knock at the door. It had to be Rose, who had probably gone through the rest of the photos.

It was Rose, but instead of her phone she was holding a plate with what looked to be some kind of breakfast sandwich.

"Is that for me?" I asked.

"It is," she said with a smile.

"Bless you. Good morning. Come in," I said, taking the plate from her. I stepped aside and Rose came into the living room.

Elvis looks up from his food, murped a hello and went back to eating.

"Good morning, Elvis," she said.

I had already taken a bite of the sandwich—scrambled egg with dill and something else, thinly sliced tomato, a slice of Havarti cheese all on a warm cheese-and-cornmeal scone. It was delicious.

"Thank you, this is so good," I mumbled around a second bite.

"I'm glad you like it," Rose said.

"Have you had a chance to look at the rest of the photos?" I asked.

She nodded. "I did and there are a couple of one of the catalytic converters that are even better than the ones we found last night. Or I guess I should say early this morning."

"I think we should show them to Mr. P. and see if he thinks we have enough to go to the police."

"That will mean telling him what we did. Are you comfortable with that?"

I thought for a moment. "I am," I said. I'd kept Rose safe. I didn't think Mr. P. would have any quibble with our little stakeout. "And weren't you going to tell him after the fact anyway?"

"I was. I am," she said. "I don't like keeping secrets from Alf." She headed for the door. "Fifteen minutes?"

Elvis lifted his head and meowed.

I did some quick mental math. "Elvis is right," I said. "Better make it twenty."

"I'll be ready," she said.

I held up the remaining half of my sandwich. "Thank you for this."

"You're welcome, sweet girl," she said with a smile and left.

I got a glass of milk to have with the rest of the sandwich because I knew I didn't have time to make coffee and drink it. I took some consolation in knowing Mac would have a cup waiting for me.

Exactly twenty minutes later I came out of the apartment with Elvis just as Rose came out of her own door. As we drove to the shop with Elvis on the seat between us watching the road, I asked Rose what she knew about Addie and Cherry Glover.

"Not a lot, really. That little house is the house they grew up in. They're very private people."

"That's understandable, given their third side business," I said.

Rose smiled. "But at the same time they've been very generous to causes like the hot lunch program and the fund-raising campaign for the sunflower window."

"I keep wondering if Michael had figured out what was happening next door."

"We figured it out pretty quickly, so I don't see how he could have remained in the dark. "

"He didn't call the police, at least as far as we know," I said, waiting for a minivan to go by so I could turn left.

"I think it's pretty clear he didn't, because the transactions wouldn't still be going on if he had," Rose said.

I glanced over at her. She was giving Elvis a scratch under his chin with one hand.

"Do you think Addie and Cherry had anything to do with his death—intentionally or impulsively?"

She made a face, her mouth twisting to one side for a moment. "I hate to think that what seem like two nice people could have done that, but as we've both learned, nice people do bad things more often than we like to think."

As usual Mac had coffee waiting for me, and Mr. P. was already in the Angels' office working at his computer.

"Good morning," he said, smiling at Rose. "I made the tea."

"Thank you, Alf," she said. She touched my arm. "Just give me a minute," she said softly. I nodded.

As soon as Rose left the room I cleared my throat, which got both Mac and Mr. P.'s attention. "Rose and I came across some information last night that may have something to do with our case," I said. "As soon as Rose comes back down we'll explain."

"I look forward to hearing what you've learned," Mr. P. said. He turned back to his computer.

"Does this have something to do with your visit to the man Michael Norris evicted?" Mac asked.

I shook my head. "He has an alibi. And I'm a little bit in love with his house." I explained about Tyrell's colorful living room and his colorful personality. "What about you? Any luck with the trailer?" Mac had gone to look at a boat trailer. At some point the boat had to come out of Memphis's garage.

"No. Too big and too expensive. I'll keep looking." He took a sip of his coffee. "But I did get some great news about an hour ago. As long as he doesn't get bumped again, Jameis will be here tonight. His flight is scheduled to land in Portland at suppertime and I'll pick him up."

"Yay!" I said, doing a little fist pump. "I'm so glad I'm finally getting to meet Jameis in the flesh. I know we've talked a lot via video call, but this will be so much better."

Mac smiled. "It will. It's been too long since I've spent time with my little brother. He's only going to be here for a few days, but I want to make the most of it."

I smiled at him over the top of my coffee mug. "Take off whatever time you need while Jameis is here. We can work around you."

"Thanks," he said.

Rose came in carrying a cup of tea and nodded at

me. I set my mug on the table, wiped my hands on my pants and looked at Mac and Mr. P.

"When Rose talked to Merton at the dentist's office he said something that stuck in her mind," I said. I looked at Mr. P. "He said the same thing to you. He mentioned that Michael Norris was considered a bit of a prickly person by some of his neighbors, in particular the Glover sisters, who live right next door."

"What exactly was the problem?" Mr. P. asked. "Merton didn't go into any details."

Rose explained about Michael's complaints about cars and visitors late at night.

"That doesn't sound like a reason to kill someone," Mac said. "Just more like the usual sort of neighbor conflict when a quiet person lives next to a more social person."

"I agree," Rose said. "But what little I could glean about Addie and Cherry Glover didn't fit with them having friends over all the time and late at night to boot. And they don't have a lot of family. It seemed a little out of character."

I nodded. "The more Rose and I talked about it, the more it struck us as strange so we decided to drive over and look around."

Mr. P. frowned. "I would have been happy to accompany you. You could have called me."

"I know that, Alf," Rose said, "but we only intended to cruise around the neighborhood a little."

Mac and Mr. P. exchanged a look. "I take it the two of you did a little more than that," Mac said.

I nodded again. "Yes, we did. It was quiet and most of the houses were in darkness but there was a light on in the Glover house so we parked and watched the place for a few minutes."

Mr. P. took off his glasses, took out the little cloth he carried in his pocket and began the careful ritual of cleaning the lenses. "Would I be correct in assuming you saw something?"

"Yes, you would," Rose said. "In a very short period of time we saw three different people unload something large from their vehicles, put whatever it was in the sisters' backyard and receive cash from a roll of money Addie Glover had in her pocket."

"Seriously?" Mac asked.

"Seriously," I said.

"So these people were selling something?"

"It looks that way," I said. I took another sip of my coffee. "From where we were watching—which, before either of you ask, was far enough away not to be noticed—we couldn't tell what that something was, other than it seemed heavy. The merchandise was always covered with some kind of tarp."

"What did you do?" Mr. P. asked, putting his glasses back on again.

"I slipped into Michael's yard and took some photos under the fence of the Glovers' backyard," I said. I held up one hand. "And then we came home. No confrontations with anyone." I decided the conversation about my "lost" dog couldn't really be called a confrontation.

"And I stayed in Sarah's SUV the entire time," Rose said.

Mac raised his eyebrows in surprise.

Rose pointed a finger at him. "I saw that," she said.

He smiled. "I know you did."

"And what is the merchandise?" Mr. P. asked. "I'm assuming you know now."

I looked at Rose and gestured at Mr. P. She handed him her phone. "Catalytic converters," I said.

Mac leaned over to look at the photos as well. Mr. P. nodded. "For the platinum and rhodium."

"That's our guess," I said.

"It doesn't necessarily mean the Glover sisters had anything to do with Michael Norris's death," Mr. P. said.

Rose nodded. "No, it doesn't, but it does put the two of them on our radar."

"Those photos need to go to Michelle," I said.

"I agree," Mr. P. said, "but perhaps they should do so via Joshua. They were taken during an investigation we're engaged in for his office."

Mac ran a hand back over his hair. "I'm with Alfred."

Rose and I looked at each other. After a moment she nodded. "That's fine with us," I said.

"I can download the images onto my computer and we can find the best ones," Mr. P. said. "I don't think Michelle is going to ask too many questions about who took the photos and how."

There was a knock on the back door then. "That's Charlotte," I said.

"I'll let her in," Rose said.

Mr. P. was already downloading the photos.

Mac came over to me and set his mug on the table. "You could have called me, you know," he said.

I smiled. "I know, but I really did think we were just going to make a couple of passes down the street to satisfy Rose's curiosity and then come home."

He gave me a look of skepticism.

I ducked my head for a moment. "Okay, kind of naïve of me."

"I have to ask. How did you get Rose to stay in the car? Rope? Duct tape? A large Doberman?" He held up one hand. "No, wait. She would have won it over with homemade dog biscuits."

"Actually I used a little logic and a couple of threats, believe it or not."

Mac smiled. "I'll file that away for future use." His smile faded. "Do you think those women had anything to do with Michael Norris's death?"

"I don't want to," I said. "It seems to me there's a big difference between buying stolen car parts for the precious metal they contain and killing someone."

There were two customers waiting when we unlocked the front door and that seemed to set the tone for the rest of the day. Just after nine Mac and I left to look at Jon Everly's aunt's house. It was filled with furniture and decorative items on both floors and in the basement and in the attic. Beautiful antiques sat next to inexpensive pine pieces.

"It looks as though the woman never threw anything out," Mac whispered to me.

I made notes and took photos on every floor. We'd done this type of cleanout before, but never in a house this large or this cluttered.

"It's going to take me a couple of days or so to come up with an estimate for you," I told Jon Everly.

"That's fine," he said. He looked around the front parlor, where we were standing. "This is far more than I can take on, just putting in the time on nights and weekends. And my mother could never tackle this all on her own."

"That's not something we haven't heard before," I said. "If you do decide to hire us, I'll need you to label anything the family wants to keep before we get started. Or just take photos and give us those. If we find anything we think might have sentimental value, or be worth a huge amount of money, we'll ask, but otherwise we will dispose of things according to the terms you agree on when you hire us. We do try to send as little as possible to the landfill."

Jon smiled. "I'm glad to hear that."

When Mac and I got back to the shop Mr. P. beckoned me into the office. A pen and a yellow legal pad were next to his computer. I could see that he'd written down all the names we'd gotten from Glenn and Jo-anna Norris as well as several others.

"I've managed to eliminate two of the names from our list of people who were at the party," he said. "One lived in Australia for the last ten years and died in a car accident six months ago. Her name was Elyse Tremblay. And the other has been traveling in Europe for the past three weeks." He sighed. "I confess that I feel a small twinge of envy after seeing the woman's photos of Venice."

I held out both hands. "Are you saying you'd give up all of this for Venice?"

He smiled. "Well, not permanently, but for three weeks I wouldn't take much persuading." He glanced at the list on the desk. "I've also located one of the remaining four party attendees. His name is Simon Kang. He's a community college instructor in South Portland."

I smiled. "Road trip?"

"Not this time," Mr. P. said. "Simon Kang has been here in North Harbor for several weeks, working on the new AP math program that's being instituted at Avery's school in the fall."

"He sounds like someone we should talk to," I said.

Mr. P. nodded. "I'm wondering if perhaps Elizabeth might be the best person to talk to Mr. Kang."

"Given the fact that Liz has been a very generous donor to every fund-raiser the school has had since Avery has been a student there, she probably wouldn't have any problem getting past the front door."

"The administration, at least, does have some affection for her," he said.

"Would you like me to go with Liz?" I asked.

"I would, if you don't mind. I think that the two of you make a formidable team. I will call Jane and see if Elizabeth is available as soon as this afternoon."

"Okay," I said. "Let me know what she says." I pulled a hand over my neck and blew out a breath.

"Is something wrong?" Mr. P. asked.

"Not really," I said. "It's just that I feel a bit like

we're throwing darts in the general direction of a dartboard with the hope that if we throw enough, eventually we'll hit a bull's-eye. Glenn has no alibi for the time of Michael's death. He was at the shop but it was closed so there's no one to confirm that. More than one witness saw the two of them arguing that morning and we know Glenn had a reason to be angry at Michael. Plus he knew about Michael's sesame seed allergy, which we're still not certain is what killed him."

"Sarah, are you familiar with the infinite monkey theorem?" he said. "It goes back as far as Aristotle."

"I am. A monkey, randomly hitting keys on a typewriter for an infinite amount of time, will eventually type every piece of text ever written including everything Shakespeare produced."

He nodded.

"I'm sorry. The analogy isn't helping. We don't have an infinite amount of time."

Mr. P. smiled. "That's true, but we're also not monkeys and we're not just randomly hitting typewriter keys. We're looking for answers. We will figure it out."

"How do you know?"

"Because we always do."

"So a self-fulfilling prophecy."

He nodded. "In a way, yes."

"Okay," I said. "I'll try a little harder to have a little faith." I got to the doorway and turned back to look at him. "I would like to point out that when a group of grad students in England set up a group of monkeys with a keyboard they did *not* produce the complete works of Shakespeare. In fact one monkey hit the keyboard with a rock, which I admit I have had the urge to do myself more than once, and a couple of the others chose to urinate on the keys."

Mr. P. pushed his glasses up his nose. "Well, I certainly hope this case doesn't come to that," he said.

I laughed all the way back to my office.

Chapter 18

Half an hour later Mr. P. tapped on my office door. "I found Emily Young," he said without preamble.

I gave him a blank look.

"Emily is one of the two students Freddie Black failed. She lives in Seattle now. I have a video call with her in five minutes." He glanced at his watch. "Actually more like four minutes now. Would you like to join me?"

I'd made good progress on the estimate for Jon Everly. I could take a little break. "I would," I said, getting to my feet.

The moment I saw Emily Young I knew she wasn't our killer. She had blue eyes, brown hair pulled back in a low ponytail and she was hugely pregnant. There was no way she could have flown across the country so close to her due date and I couldn't imagine she would have driven, either.

"When's the baby due?" I asked.

She patted her belly. "Friday," she said with a

smile. She brushed a stray strand of hair off her face and addressed Mr. P. "You said in your email that you had some questions about Freddie Black. That's a name I haven't heard in years. She taught a math tutorial I was in, but I'm guessing you knew that."

"I did," Mr. P. said.

"So you probably found out I almost failed the class."

Mr. P. and I exchanged a look. "Almost?" he said.

Emily smiled again. "Freddie gave Ronan—Ronan Killam; he failed as well—and me a chance to make up the failure, to do some extra coursework."

"That I didn't know," Mr. P. said.

"Freddie had what my dad would call a 'strong personality.' When she made up her mind about something you'd have about as much chance of changing it as you would have had arguing with a tree. She didn't have to give either one of us that second chance, and honestly, I was surprised she did. In my case, I'd been spending too much time on my social life and not enough on studying. I think it was pretty much the same with Ronan." Emily looked away from the screen for a moment. "It was the day that she died, you know, that she called with the news. Then the party happened and she was gone."

She looked at us again. "You said you're looking into Michael Norris's death."

"Yes, we are," Mr. P. said.

"What does that have to do with what happened to Freddie? Andrew Lewis went to prison for killing her."

"Maybe nothing," Mr. P. said. "At this point we

don't know. The only connection we have so far is that Michael died on that same stretch of beach."

She shook her head slowly. "I can't believe he was there. I never went back there again and Michael knew Freddie a lot better than I did."

I glanced at Mr. P. His eyes narrowed behind his wire-framed glasses. He'd noticed Emily had said "again" just as I had. Did it mean what I thought it meant?

"Emily, were you at the party that night?" I asked.

"I was," she said. "Back then I had a thing for Glenn McNamara, who pretty much didn't seem to know I was alive. I had way too much to drink and tried to get Michael to kiss me, thinking somehow that would make Glenn jealous and then he'd fall madly in love with me. And yes, I know how stupid that sounds but I was twenty-one."

I gave her a wry smile. "Been there. Done that. More than once."

"Well, for the record, it didn't work. Michael was acting weird—jumpy. Finally he stood up, said that he was going for a walk and headed up the beach. So I made out with some other drunk guy." Her expression changed. "I think we all drank too much back then. Maybe if we hadn't, Freddie would be alive." She rubbed her baby bump. "I wish I could help you. Have you talked to Ronan yet? We stay in touch. He's back living in North Harbor. He's the new executive chef at The Elms."

The Elms was a luxury resort about halfway between North Harbor and Camden. The new owners were renovating the property with a soft reopening planned for the end of June.

"Ronan and his wife are getting settled in and he's working on a new menu for the main restaurant. He bought a little cottage on Mill Street. Do you know that wonderful repurpose shop, Second Chance? He's about halfway up the hill from there."

I grinned at her. "As a matter of fact, I do." I held out both hands. "I own Second Chance. It's where we are right now."

Emily laughed. "Small world. My mother bought a bed frame from you and some Blue Willow dishes a couple of months ago."

We sold a lot of Blue Willow china—it was popular with collectors—but the image of a tall, slender woman with cropped gray hair and the same smile as Emily came to me. "Your mother is Dinah Young," I said.

Emily nodded. "She is." She looked around. "I'm sorry I couldn't help you, but as soon as I find my phone I'll send you Ronan's contact information. He wasn't at the party but I think Freddie talked to him in person about our makeup assignments. Maybe she said something that might help you."

Mr. P. thanked her and we said good-bye.

I leaned back in my chair and eyed Mr. P. "Liz won't be here for a couple of hours."

"You're correct," he said.

"Charlotte is here, Mac is here and Ronan Killam is only about five minutes away."

"Also correct," he said.

"I think the universe is sending us a message."

Mr. P. smiled then. "Well, who am I to argue with the universe."

I told Mac and Charlotte where we were going and why, grabbed my bag, and Mr. P. and I got in my SUV. I had a pretty good idea which house Emily had talked about. It was actually one I'd looked at before I bought my old Victorian.

We found the house and what had to be Ronan Killam in the front yard, weeding a flower bed. He looked younger than midthirties, which I realized he had to be. He had thick, dark hair, cut short on the sides and back. He was about average height and build with strong arms and a warm smile.

"I'm Alfred Peterson," Mr. P. said, offering his business card. "This is Sarah Grayson. I'm a private investigator looking into the death of Michael Norris. Emily Young suggested we talk to you about Freddie Black."

Ronan smiled. "Has Emily had the baby yet?"

Mr. P. shook his head. "Not unless it happened in the last fifteen minutes."

Ronan gestured at a round glass-and-metal table behind him. There were four wooden chairs with beige strap-style webbing spaced around it. The chairs were new. The table was vintage and in excellent shape. Ronan Killam or someone had excellent taste.

"How about a glass of lemonade?" Ronan offered. "I made it myself."

Mr. P. smiled. "Yes, please."

Ronan looked at me.

I nodded. "I'd love to try it. Thank you."

"I'll be right back," he said.

"I almost bought this house," I said to Mr. P. as we sat down. "Before I bought mine. It's had quite a bit of work done since the last time I was here."

The house had a new roof and new clapboards. The oversize porch on the front that had listed badly to the right was gone. I remembered the tiny bathroom inside with a tub so small anyone past the age of six wouldn't have been able to stretch out their legs in it.

Mr. P. looked around. "I may be biased but I like the house you have."

"So do I," I said. The cottage reminded me of a little dollhouse. There would be no room for Gram and John, or Rose, and I knew I would miss having them close by.

Ronan returned with our lemonade. I wondered if he'd offered it as a gesture of hospitality or to give himself a few minutes to organize his thoughts about Freddie.

I took a sip. "This is delicious," I said.

Ronan smiled. "Thank you. I make a honey syrup to sweeten the drink. It adds a lot of flavor."

Mr. P. took another drink, a thoughtful expression on his face. "May I ask where you get your honey?" he said. "Would it be Forget-Me-Not Farms, just up the coast, by any chance?"

Ronan nodded. "As a matter of fact, yes. Their wildflower honey is some of the best I've ever tasted." He set his glass down. "So you want to talk about Freddie Black."

"We do," Mr. P. said.

Ronan raked a hand back through his hair. "You probably already know I was in a tutorial she taught."

Mr. P. nodded.

"I'm guessing you also know she failed Emily and me," Ronan said.

"We know that as well," Mr. P. said.

"And since you've already talked to Emily you probably know that both of us deserved it. We missed too many classes and we turned in more than one assignment late." He turned his glass in a slow circle on the table. "I don't really have a good excuse for my behavior, just too much wine, women and song—substituting cheap beer for wine."

"'Who loves not women, wine and song, remains a fool his whole life long,'" Mr. P. said, "attributed to Martin Luther without any definitive substantiation."

Ronan laughed. "I'll remember that." His smile faded. "Freddie was a good instructor. Everyone in the class liked her. She's the one who convinced Dr. Singh—he was the prof—to let us do a couple more assignments for extra credit so we could pass. I have no idea why. He wasn't exactly warm and fuzzy, but she persuaded him. I don't know what she said to Emily when she told her, but in my case at least, she told me not to blow it. I couldn't believe it when I heard the next day that she was dead."

"Do you remember anything else about the conversation?" I asked.

He shook his head. "I don't. It was just chance that I bumped into her. I was working the breakfast shift at Ernie's Diner. I was on my way home. We talked for maybe three minutes."

"Were you at the party that night?" Mr. P. asked.

Emily had said he wasn't but I was guessing Mr. P. wanted to hear Ronan's answer.

"No. I was out with some of my buddies celebrating." His gaze shifted between the two of us. "Do either of you remember a bar called the Blue Lagoon?"

We both nodded. The term "dive bar" had been created for the Blue Lagoon.

"Not exactly a high-end establishment," Ronan said, "but the beer was cheap. "It's possible there's video somewhere of me singing karaoke that night to 'Livin' on a Prayer.'"

"We'll keep our eyes and ears open for that," Mr. P. said, a hint of a smile pulling up the corners of his mouth.

"Do you mind telling us where you were last Wednesday?" I asked.

Ronan shook his head and reached for his phone. He tapped the screen a couple of times, swiped and then turned it around for us to see. A photo of Ronan surrounded by a small group of people filled the screen. A large casserole dish of what looked to be bread pudding was on a countertop in front of them.

"I was teaching a cooking class in Portland," he said. "At Rankin House. I wasn't with Michael Norris. I barely knew him."

Rankin House was a four-star boutique hotel in downtown Portland.

Ronan frowned. "You don't think there's some sort

of connection between Freddie's death and what happened to Michael Norris?"

"Do you?" Mr. P. asked.

"No. I don't. Why would there be?"

"They both died at the same place," I said.

"Fifteen years apart. What was he was doing down there anyway?"

Mr. P. nudged his glasses up his nose. "That's what we're trying to find out."

"Do you think he was meeting someone?"

"It's possible," I said.

"It wasn't me," Ronan said. "Like you saw from the photo, I was in Portland making white chocolate and raspberry bread pudding. And I'm surprised Michael was anywhere near that stretch of beach."

"Why do you say that?" Mr. P. asked.

I knew what Ronan's answer was going to be before he spoke.

"Michael and Freddie were friends. Why would he go back to the place where she died, where she was murdered? It seems to me that would be the last place he'd want to meet someone. Whatever his reason was for being on that beach has to be a damn good one."

There wasn't anything else to say. We thanked Ronan for talking to us and for the lemonade and walked back down the driveway.

"He confirmed everything Emily told us," I said once I'd fastened my seat belt.

"I assumed he would," Mr. P. said. "Neither Emily nor Ronan had any reason to kill Freddie and they both have alibis for Michael's death—which I'll confirm."

"I knew you would," I said as I pulled away from the curb. I glanced over at him as we headed down the hill. "Why was Michael on that stretch of beach?"

"I don't know," he said, "but the answer is out there."

I shook my head. "The question is, where?"

Chapter 19

When we got back to Second Chance, Mr. P. reminded me that Liz would be arriving at two o'clock so she and I could go talk to Simon Kang.

"What do you need to know?" I asked. Rose had joined us in the office.

"Ask him what he remembers from the night Freddie Black died," Rose said. "See if he's stayed in touch with anybody. And it would help to know what he was doing when Michael Norris died."

Avery showed up a quarter to twelve. She was wearing her usual black jeans and Docs with a gray T-shirt that said **English Is Important But Math Is Importanter** across the front.

"English exam today?" I said.

"Yeah," she said. "How did you know?"

"Lucky guess," I said, trying not to smile. "So how would you feel about working full-time over the summer?"

"You mean it?"

I nodded. "Yes. I'm hoping we'll get a big job clearing out someone's house and I could use you."

"For sure. Yes." She twisted the leather cuff she was wearing around her wrist. "Greg is going to be working as a lifeguard, which means he'll be working weekends and he'll have a couple of days off during the week and a couple of mornings as well. I know he's looking to make as much money as he can before college starts in the fall. I mean, if you need any extra help with that house and all."

"We probably could use an extra set of hands and a strong back at least while we're clearing out the house," I said. "Next time Greg comes to meet you at the end of the day tell him to come find me."

Avery smiled. "I will for sure."

I spent the next couple of hours on Jon Everly's estimate. Liz arrived a few minutes before two o'clock. She looked a little intimidating in navy trousers and a navy jacket over a purple blouse and of course her ubiquitous high heels. I was glad I had dressed a little nicer than usual because of the meeting with Jon Everly.

Liz looked me over and I found myself standing up straighter. "You'll do," she said.

"You too," I replied.

Liz turned her attention to Rose. "Have you found where Andrew Lewis is working yet?"

"He's been hard to track down." Rose seemed just a little defensive. I wondered if she'd asked Nick about Andrew. Law enforcement would know he was back in North Harbor.

"I don't doubt that because he's changed his name,"

Liz said. "He's going by his middle name now, Hayden, which was his mother's maiden name. He's working at Pine Knoll Farm."

"The cheese maker that Alf likes at the market," Rose said. "How on earth did you manage to track him down?"

Liz smiled. "People like to stay on my good side. So they like to tell me things."

"Well . . . thank you," Rose said. There was a bit of tightness in her voice.

Liz made a hurry-up gesture in my direction. "Let's roll," she said.

She headed for the door. Rose blew me a kiss.

We started across the parking lot to Liz's car. "I could drive," I said.

"And why in heaven's name would I let you drive my new car?" Liz said.

"Because I'm a safe and responsible driver."

Liz gave a snort of laughter. "Good one," she said. "Try again."

"Because I really, really, really want to and you looovve me."

Liz shook her head, but she handed over the keys.

I gave a squeal of happiness and jumped up and down.

"Are you six?" she said.

"I feel like it at the moment," I said, grinning at her. I let Liz in on the passenger side, then walked around and opened the driver's door, running my hand over the back of the seat before sitting down. I checked the wipers, mirrors, turn signals and fan before I started the car.

I drove to Avery's school, which was up the hill from the shop, about a twenty-minute walk and a much shorter drive. I didn't go even half a mile over the speed limit, even though I was itching to see what the car could do. I kept my eyes on the road and pulled into a parking spot at the school where I could drive directly out, because I knew if anything happened to Liz's car I would have to change my name and go live in a research station in Antarctica.

As we got out of the car I noticed a silver Audi in the lot with a Southern Maine Community College parking sticker in the window. That was where Simon Kang taught. I wondered if the car was his.

"Let me do the talking," Liz said as we headed for the front door.

"I was planning on it," I said.

There was a security officer at the entrance. He was built like a hockey goalie, short and stocky with huge hands. "Hello, Mrs. French," he said with a smile. "Are you headed to the administration office?"

"Yes, Jason, we are," she said. "This is Sarah Grayson."

"Good afternoon, Ms. Grayson," he said. He let us into the building.

Liz's footsteps echoed down the wide hallway of the old brick building. I knew it had been some kind of textile manufacturing plant a century ago and had had several other incarnations before it became the rather unconventional private school that Avery had been attending.

The school office looked like every other school office I had ever seen. The walls were painted a pale shade of green. An oversized bulletin board was covered in notices and flyers. A woman in her early forties, I guessed, was behind the counter. She looked up and smiled when she recognized Liz.

"Mrs. French, hello," she said.

Liz smiled back. "Hello, Penny," she said. "How's your wrist? I see the cast is gone."

I noticed a brace on the woman's left arm.

She smiled. "It's a lot better now that that awkward cast is off. Thank you for the muffins. I was feeling very sorry for myself the morning they arrived."

"You're very welcome," Liz said. "I've found that a blueberry muffin or a lemon square will certainly improve my mood."

Behind her I smiled and nodded my head.

"How may I help you?" Penny asked.

Liz gestured at me. "This is Sarah, my assistant. We just need to talk to Simon Kang for a few minutes, please."

"He should be up on level two in the math lab."

Liz nodded. "I know where that is." She thanked Penny and we headed back down the hall to a wide stairwell at the end.

"Assistant?" I said once we were out of earshot of the office.

Liz quirked one eyebrow at me. "Would you rather I said chauffer?" she asked.

"No. But couldn't I have been your associate?"

"No one would believe you're my associate dressed like that."

I looked down at my gray-checked pants and blue shirt. "What's wrong with how I'm dressed?"

"Nothing," Liz said. "If you're an assistant."

We started up the stairs to the second floor.

"Could I have a cool hat?" I asked.

Liz frowned at me. "For what?"

"So you could introduce me as your chauffer. No one would believe it without a hat."

"Next time I'm going to leave you behind and I won't have to introduce you as anything," Liz said, but I knew she wasn't really annoyed at me. She couldn't quite hide her smile.

"Why didn't Penny ask why you wanted to talk to Simon Kang?" I asked. "Avery won't be a student here next year."

"Probably because she knows who's funding this fancy new math program Mr. Kang is helping put together."

I leaned over and kissed her cheek, careful not to leave any lipstick imprint behind. "You're one of my favorite people," I said.

"Flattery does not work on me, missy."

"You can you call it flattery, but it's still the truth."

Liz shook her head. "Why do I put up with you?"

"Because I'm one of your favorite people."

"Heaven help me, you are," she said. Liz paused at the top of the steps. "I never thought I'd say this but this school has been good for Avery."

"Living with you has been good for Avery," I said.

Liz smiled. "For me, too, and in truth I'm glad she won't be that far away come fall." She pointed a finger at me. "Do not tell anyone I said that."

I mimed zipping my mouth shut.

"She'll stay in the dorm all week and come back

most weekends, at least that's the plan. Hard to believe, but the child wants to be here for the weekends."

"She's already asked about working Saturdays, in
the fall," I said.

"All of you have been good for Avery."

I smiled back at her. "She's been good for us."

Liz pointed at a door halfway down the hall.
"That's the math lab," she said.

"So what are we going to do?" I asked.

"Find out what Mr. Kang remembers from the
night Freddie Black died and see if he killed Michael
Norris."

"You can't just ask him that last part," I said.

Liz squared her shoulders and smiled in a way that
made me think of a shark. "Watch and learn," she
said.

Inside the math lab a man was working at a large
Mac computer. He looked up at us. "Can I help you?"
he said. He had Asian ancestry with straight, dark
hair cut short. His eyes were dark brown behind
semi-rimless eyeglass frames with a gunmetal finish
and he was wearing jeans and a white shirt with the
sleeves rolled back. What caught my eye immediately
was the vintage Longines watch on his left arm. It
was from the mid 1960s, I guessed, with a silvered
face, a seconds indicator and a brown leather strap
that I doubted was original. My best guess was that
the watch would sell for more than a thousand dollars on the resale market. Simon Kang, if this was
him, had good taste, at least in watches. And possibly
an affluent background—or maybe I was jumping to
conclusions.

"Are you Simon Kang?" Liz asked.

"Yes, I am," he said. "And you are?"

"I'm Elizabeth French."

He got to his feet with a last glance at his computer screen and came around the desk holding out his hand. "From the Emmerson Foundation," he said. They shook hands.

Points to Mr. Kang for recognizing her name, I thought.

"This is Sarah Grayson. My *associate*," Liz said.

"Nice to meet you," he said, and again offered his hand. Then he turned his attention back to Liz. "What can I do for you, Mrs. French?"

"Almost fifteen years ago you went to a party where a young woman named Freddie Black died. Just last week Michael Norris lost his life along that same stretch of beach." Liz did not beat around the bush.

"Yes, I was at that party," Simon said. His long fingers played with the strap of his watch.

"And you and Michael Norris were friends." It was a statement, not a question.

"Michael and I were friends back when we were in college. After that we didn't really stay in touch, but I was sorry to hear that he had died."

"I've known Glenn McNamara since he was a little boy," Liz said. "The past few days there have been some rumors going around about him and what happened to Michael Norris that I don't like, and that certainly aren't true."

Simon frowned. "Are you suggesting Michael didn't drown? Do you think there's some connection between the two deaths?"

"I don't know," she said. "Do you?"

I noticed he continued to fiddle with his watch-strap, almost as though he didn't realize he was doing it. "Mrs. French, Andrew Lewis went to prison for killing Freddie. He couldn't have had anything to do with Michael's death."

"And now Andrew Lewis is out of prison."

A tiny twitch started to pulse at the corner of Simon's right eye. "I . . . I didn't know that." He finally stopped playing with his watch. He stuffed one hand in his pocket and put the other one flat on the desk. "I doubt that Andrew would have been stupid enough to commit another murder the moment he got out of jail. And what could he have had against Michael to make him want to hurt him?"

"There were two witnesses who were going to testify against Mr. Lewis before he took the plea deal," Liz said. Her gaze never wavered from Simon's face.

"Michael wasn't one of them," he said. "And those rumors about Glenn McNamara are nothing more than speculation. Unfounded speculation. Michael and I met in high school but he and Glenn had been friends since they were little kids. I didn't really know Glenn very well, but you don't kill someone you have that kind of a connection with. I think it's admirable that you want to stand up for someone you care about but there's no way anyone can seriously think Glenn McNamara had anything to do with Michael's death."

"Where were you Wednesday afternoon and evening?" Liz asked.

"I was right here, reviewing one particular section of the new curriculum again in preparation for a meeting Thursday morning. And just to be clear I hadn't seen or spoken to Michael since the day Andrew Lewis was arrested. We weren't exactly friends anymore, but I didn't kill him." He cleared his throat. "Now, if you'll excuse me, I really need to get back to work."

Liz gave him a long appraising look. "Thank you," she said and we left.

She didn't say anything more until we got to the top of the stairs. Then she looked at me. "Is it just me or was Mr. Kang nervous?"

"Well, it could be you, because you are a little intimidating, but yes he was definitely nervous. And he went out of his way to defend Glenn even though he also said he really didn't know him."

She nodded. "I noticed that as well."

I was going over everything Simon had said in my mind and I made it all the way back to the car on autopilot before I realized that I hadn't said another word to Liz.

"Something caught your attention. What was it?"

I pushed my hair back and shook my head. "It might be nothing."

"Yes, it might be, but what is it that's bothering you?"

"Simon said that Michael wasn't going to testify against Andrew."

Liz nodded. "That's what he said."

"How did he know? He told us he hadn't seen Michael since the day Andrew Lewis was arrested. So how did he know whether Michael was or wasn't going to be a witness? There was no trial because Andrew took an Alford plea so nobody testified against him. And why would Michael have testified? He hadn't told anyone what he'd seen."

I started the car and we headed for the shop. Suddenly I had it. "The grand jury," I said.

"What grand jury?" Liz said.

"I'm almost positive I read somewhere that Andrew Lewis was indicted by a grand jury."

"Which means what, exactly?"

"Simon knew who would likely testify at Andrew's trial because he knew who had testified before the grand jury. He was there. I think Simon testified before that grand jury. He was one of the two witnesses who put Freddie Black and Andrew together, arguing on that breakwater."

"It's a reach," Liz said, "but given how fidgety he was, I think you're on to something. It seems Mr. Kang knows more than he has given us to believe."

"I think so," I said.

"More importantly, will this help Glenn?"

I sighed. "That I don't know."

Chapter 20

We drove back to the shop. I got out of the car and handed Liz her keys.

"I'm not sure what we got from this," Liz said.

"Mr. P. always says that solving a case is like putting together a jigsaw puzzle. You don't always know how all the pieces are going to fit together, but eventually they will."

"I don't do jigsaw puzzles," Liz said. "Or Wordle, or Gurgle or any of those word games. Give me the *New York Times* crossword puzzle. That takes brains."

I laughed, thanked Liz for letting me drive and gave her a kiss.

"Later, toots," she said.

Mr. P. was standing in the office doorway waiting for me. "How did it go?" he asked.

I shrugged. "I'm not sure." I followed him back into the office and related Liz's conversation with Simon Kang. "I think Simon knows more than he let on to us," I said. "I think he testified in front of the grand jury. I think he was one of the witnesses that saw Andrew Lewis and Freddie Black arguing."

"What do you know about the grand jury process?" Mr. P. said.

"Not a lot."

"Secrecy is paramount to the process. It protects the innocent from anyone finding out they're under investigation, and it protects witnesses from being threatened or pressured. The rule of secrecy applies to everyone except the witnesses."

I frowned. "So what does that mean, exactly?"

"If you're a witness and you're called to testify before a grand jury, you can tell anyone what you said and what you heard during your time in front of the grand jury, including the person who is the subject of the investigation."

"So if Simon did testify he's not breaking any laws by telling us he did?"

Mr. P. shook his head. "No, he isn't, and it does make sense that Simon knows Michael isn't the unidentified second witness because *he* is."

"So let's say he is the mysterious second witness. How does that help us?"

"It could help establish a better timeline for Freddie Black's death. It could, in theory, raise reasonable doubt when put together with what Michael says he saw."

I held up one hand. "You've lost me," I said.

He smiled. "Let's see if I can make this make sense for you. I'm Simon Kang. I see Freddie and Andrew out on the breakwater arguing but I don't pay a lot of attention to them."

"I'm with you so far."

"I walk away from that part of the beach and I see someone leaving or pizza being delivered, anything that fixes that point at least somewhat in time."

"Okay," I said. I still didn't see where he was going.

"Now I'm Michael Norris. I see Freddie and someone other than Andrew out on the breakwater arguing. Again, like Simon, I don't think it's a big deal. I walk down the beach and think I'll have some pizza but it's all been eaten. Or perhaps no one has ordered pizza yet, so I find out what everyone wants and call in the order."

I began to slowly nod my head. "I get it. In your scenario if Michael sees Freddie and the other person arguing after the pizza has been eaten, that could help Andrew Lewis establish reasonable doubt."

"There are a lot of what-ifs and maybes in this kind of thing," Mr. P. said. "Maybe Simon isn't the missing witness. Or maybe he has no idea when he saw what he saw. Maybe Michael didn't, either."

"But maybe they did," I said.

He nodded. "Maybe they did."

"We need to talk to Andrew Lewis," I said.

"I agree," Mr. P. said. "By the way, I talked to Dr. Singh while you were gone."

"The professor that Emily mentioned? The one who was supervising Freddie and Andrew?"

"Yes."

"That was fast," I said.

"The alumni directory was very helpful. Dr. Singh retired to Arizona. He remembered Freddie and Andrew."

I pulled a hand over the back of my neck. "Did you learn anything useful?"

"Nothing we didn't already know. He confirmed that Andrew and Freddie didn't get along. He called Freddie prickly but very smart." He raised one eyebrow. "He seemed to imply the latter mitigated the former, so much so that he was planning on meeting with Andrew to talk about him working with another professor. Dr. Singh found the constant arguing was becoming disruptive."

"If Andrew had any idea, that might have fueled his anger toward Freddie," I said.

"Or he could just as easily been happy to get away from her," Mr. P. said, "considering how contentious their relationship was."

Mac poked his head around the door then.

"I'm leaving to get Jameis," he said to me. "We'll stop in to see you when we get here."

"I can't wait," I said. "Text me from the airport."

"I will," he said and he was gone.

Mr. P. smiled. "Everyone is looking forward to meeting Mac's brother."

"It feels odd to say I feel like I know him when we've never been in the same room together," I said. "I'm glad he's finally coming." I stood up. "So what do we do now?"

"Could you drop me at the farmers' market on the way home? Rose has a piano lesson."

"You're hoping Andrew Lewis will be at the cheese place."

"I am."

"I can do one better," I said. "I'll go with you. All I

did with Liz was be there like one of those inscrutable bodyguards who stands to one side of the nefarious bad guy in a James Bond movie and never says anything, but can kill you with his bowler hat."

Mr. P. studied me for a moment. "I think you would look very distinguished in a bowler. Or perhaps a fedora."

I laughed. "I'll keep that in mind the next time Liz and I go out to talk to someone."

A small bus tour—just one vehicle—and two vans' worth of seniors heading to a weight-lifting competition in Quebec came in, one after the other about half an hour later. The seniors were all smart, funny and strong—and more than twice my age. I was surprised to hear Rose talking with a couple of the women and discover that *she* lifted weights.

"You lift weights?" I said.

"Of course," she said. "I want to stay strong as I get older."

"Should I start lifting weights regularly at the gym?" I said to Charlotte.

She smiled and patted my arm. "Maybe start by going to the gym regularly," she said.

"Or even at all," Avery commented as she headed to the workroom.

Mr. P. and I decided to go straight from work to the farmers' market.

"I want to get some lettuce and spinach from Everleigh Greenhouses and a loaf of sourdough bread," I said. "And do you remember where the bacon you bought last time came from?"

"I'll show you where I got the bacon," Mr. P. said.

"And I really do want some cheese, which will give us a chance to watch Andrew Lewis before we talk to him."

The market was only moderately busy. I got my lettuce, spinach and bread. Mr. P. also bought a loaf and we split a half pound of bacon. Then we got in line at Pine Knoll Farm's stall.

Andrew Lewis was easy to spot. I had seen his photo online and he looked the same, only older. He was fair skinned with blond hair half flecked with gray. He wore a snug-fitting, gray Henley shirt and I noticed the muscles in his arms when he reached for something. Andrew smiled and made pleasant small talk with people but I noticed how he was always watching what was happening around him, always taking stock of what was going on.

When we got to the counter I bought a quarter pound of Havarti and half a pound of mozzarella with the idea that maybe Mac would want to make lasagna while Jameis was here. Mr. P. chose his favorite Gouda and he and Andrew—whose name tag said HAYDEN—debated the merits of the four cheddar options. After he paid for his choices Mr. P. offered his business card to Andrew and explained that we were working for Glenn McNamara's lawyer.

"Would you be willing to talk to us when you have a break?" he asked.

I saw how Andrew's face closed and I found myself holding my breath, expecting him to say no.

"Why does Glenn need a lawyer?" he said instead.

"You've heard about what happened to Michael Norris," Mr. P. said.

"I did."

"That's why Glenn has a lawyer."

"Glenn McNamara wouldn't hurt anyone."

Mr. P. nodded. "We are in agreement." He held up his hand. "Five minutes, that's all."

Andrew finally gave a brief nod. "It will be about twenty minutes."

"That's fine," Mr. P. said. "They have some excellent coffee two booths down." He pointed at the seating area. "We'll wait over there."

Mr. P. and I got in line for coffee, spending a fair amount of time deciding what we wanted. I deferred to his judgment about the beans, but I managed to get my money out to pay before he did.

He wagged a finger at me. "I was going to treat you."

Our server smiled. "It's really nice of you to buy your grandfather's coffee. "

I laughed all the way to our table.

"It was very nice of you to pay for my coffee, but it would have been a little more flattering if that young woman had called you my daughter instead."

I leaned toward him and patted my cheek. "It's my new moisturizer. It makes me look ten years younger."

Mr. P. pretended to study my skin for a moment. "I can see that," he said solemnly. We both laughed.

Andrew joined us about twenty-five minutes later. I found it hard to think of him as Hayden.

"How can I help Glenn?" he asked. "He's one of the few people who stayed in touch when I went to prison—the only person from my circle of friends. And I know what it's like to be suspected of something you didn't do."

"You said you heard about Michael's death," Mr. P. said.

"I did, but I didn't hear any details," Andrew said. "In truth I've been trying to get my life on track and stay focused on that. Michael and I had been friends but that connection had disappeared when I went to jail."

"He was found in the water on the same stretch of beach where Freddie Black died," Mr. P. said.

Andrew shook his head. "That doesn't make sense. The Michael I knew didn't like the water."

"We'd heard that," I said.

"I can't imagine why anyone who was there the night Freddie died would ever want to go back there."

"What happened that night?" Mr. P. asked.

Andrew closed his eyes for a moment. "It's true that we had an argument. I thought she was too hard on the students in her tutorial section. She failed two of them, for heaven's sake. She thought I was too easy on the ones in mine. It was a statistics class that most of the students were taking because it was required, not because they had plans for a job where they'd be analyzing data. As far as I knew, not only did she fail those two students but she also refused to give them a chance to do makeup work. All they wanted was another chance—they weren't asking for a get out of jail free card." He gave us a tight smile. "Pardon the phrase."

"You argued," Mr. P. said. "Then what?"

"There's no point in lying to you. I was angry. I knew Freddie had complained to Dr. Singh about me. She called me entitled and I called her a bitch." He shook his head. "I'm always going to regret that was the last thing I said to someone who was my friend. I don't know why she didn't tell me that she'd gone to Dr. Singh and both of her students actually were getting some makeup work. Maybe she wanted me to admit I was wrong first. Anyway, I walked away, drank two beers and tried to figure out if I could switch profs. The next thing I knew, someone hollered that there was a body floating in the water." Andrew's voice was raspy with emotion. "It was Freddie."

Mr. P. patted his pocket where he kept his phone but made no move to take it out. "Did you see anyone go out on those rocks after you came back to the beach?"

Andrew shook his head. "I didn't. It might have helped my case if I had, but I didn't want to lie and put someone else in the same kind of mess I was in. You know they found my St. Christopher medal there?"

"When did you realize you'd lost it?" I asked.

"Not until I got home. The catch was loose. It had been for a while. Not that anyone believed that. What does any of this have to do with Glenn? Do the police think Freddie's death and Michael's are connected? Because I didn't see Glenn anywhere near that end of the beach. The last time I saw him he was by the bonfire, which was around the corner."

I realized he meant on Clayton's stretch of water.

"The police are, of course, not sharing the details of their investigation with anyone, but there are some signs that they believe the two deaths could be connected," Mr. P. said. "Something I doubt you're aware of is that Glenn and Michael argued the morning Michael died."

"About what?" Andrew's surprise seemed genuine.

"It seems that Michael may have kept something to himself that could possibly have established reasonable doubt in your case."

He swore and looked away. After a moment he turned back to us again. "And now that he's dead I can't use whatever that was to maybe clear my name. How did he die? Did he drown?"

"The medical examiner's office hasn't released a final report yet," I said, "but Michael had a head injury and it looks as though he may have had an allergic reaction to something he ate as well. At some point after those things happened he ended up in the water. He was likely unconscious."

Andrew swiped a hand across his face. "His allergy to sesame."

"Yes."

"But Michael always used to be so careful, paranoid actually." Then his expression changed. "You think that someone basically poisoned him, used his allergy to kill him."

"It's a possibility," Mr. P. said.

Andrew's face hardened again. "And you want to know if I have an alibi."

"Yes, we do," Mr. P. said. "Michael died last Wednesday, probably sometime between midafternoon and early evening."

Andrew laughed. "Do I have an alibi?" he said. "You might say that I have a divine alibi. I was at St. Timothy's Church all afternoon with the minister and several members of the congregation working in their community garden. They fed me supper and it was after dark when I headed back to the residence where I'm living."

Mr. P. nodded. "Thank you for telling us."

"I don't see how Freddie's death and Michael's can be connected since the main connection between the two is me, and as I just told you I have an alibi for the time of Michael's death."

"You've always maintained your innocence in Freddie's death," I said.

"That's because I *am* innocent."

"In that case, perhaps the main connection between Freddie's death and Michael's is the person who actually killed Freddie."

Chapter 21

After Andrew went back to work Mr. P. and I sat at the table a little longer.

"Are we sure that Michael's death wasn't just random?" I asked, turning my coffee cup in a circle on the table.

"I think we pretty much eliminated that idea when we found out that the hummus in his backpack had been tampered with. And there is the injury to his head."

"Okay," I said. "How did the killer get Michael out there and why that specific stretch of beach?"

"I don't have the answer to the first part of your question," Mr. P. said, "but I think the significance of the location is because somehow there's a connection to Freddie's murder."

"So if Andrew isn't responsible for Freddie's death, who is?"

"I'd love to give you a name," he said, "but I don't have one."

I leaned back in my seat and laid one hand flat on the table. "We know it wasn't Glenn because we know Glenn. And the two students Freddie failed had been given a reprieve by the professor so they had no motive. But what about Michael?"

Mr. P. tipped his head to one side, a pensive expression on his face. "That's an interesting thought."

"That's what Dad says when he's trying to be positive, but really thinks your idea is stupid."

He smiled. "I don't think your idea is stupid, but are you saying Michael killed Freddie and then after almost fifteen years and the death of Andrew's grandmother, he finally had an attack of guilt, went to the beach, ate hummus he had tampered with as a form of suicide and didn't leave a note to at least exonerate Andrew? Not to mention why did he tell Glenn he thought he could clear the man if he was going to commit suicide and keep what he knew to himself?"

"Okay, when you put it all together like that it doesn't exactly make sense," I said with a sigh. I got to my feet and reached for our empty cups. "I know you're going to say we just need a few more pieces in place and then we'll be able to see the picture."

He smiled. "I'm getting to be too predictable."

"I prefer to say you're dependable."

Mr. P. stood up as well. "As long as you don't call me Gramps," he said with a wink.

I put our cups in the garbage can and dropped the lids into the recycling bin. As we left I spotted Joanna Norris at the little bakery stall where I had gotten my sourdough bread. I wondered if Joanna knew that Andrew was working here. I also saw Glenn, with coffee and a giant bag of spinach. He waved and Mr. P. and I waved back. Just as we got to the door I noticed Simon Kang buying coffee beans. I pointed him out to Mr. P. so he could put a face to the name.

"I'm going to do a little digging into Mr. Kang when I get home," he said.

As we drove to Mr. P.'s apartment we talked about the merits of Brazilian versus Ethiopian coffee beans. I loved his enthusiasm for the subject.

"Sarah, we will figure all of this out," he said before he got out of the car. "We always have in the past."

I held up one hand with my fingers crossed.

He smiled. "That can't hurt, either."

I headed home with Elvis, who we had left snoozing in the SUV while we were at the market. I gave him his supper and then used the greens, the cheese, the bread and some cooked chicken to make a sandwich, which I grilled in my cast-iron frying pan the way Rose had taught me.

I was trying to decide which container of soup to take out of my freezer when there was a knock at the door. It was Rose with a tin of brownies for when Mac and Jameis arrived.

"You are the sweetest person I know," I said, giving her a hug.

"Thank you," she said, giving me a smile.

"How was your piano lesson?"

"Wonderful as usual. You know, it really is true that you're never too old to learn new things. Then after I was done, I stopped in to see Tabitha for a minute."

Rose's friend Tabitha still lived in Legacy Place, the seniors' building where Rose used to live.

"And how are things with Tabitha?" Tabitha and several other residents of the building were putting together a tenants group with the very grudging support of management. Rose was helping behind the scenes.

"They have a draft set of guidelines, but I expect management at Shady Pines to balk at them, and yes, I know I shouldn't call it Shady Pines. Honestly, though, they act like their tenants are a bunch of doddering old fools. It's insulting." She almost bristled with indignation.

"All true," I said, trying not to smile, "but you are not above using that assumption that seniors are doddering fools when it serves your purpose."

Her chin came up. "That's different. That's a choice."

I put an arm around her shoulders and kissed her cheek. "Rose Jackson, you are many things," I said, "smart, funny, kind, generous, devious, annoying—"

"You could have stopped after generous," she said, a smile working its way across her face.

"One thing you never will be is doddering."

I was online about an hour later, seeing what I could learn about Simon Kang with Elvis very much getting in the way, when he suddenly jumped down from my lap and headed for the door.

Mac and Jameis, I thought. I opened the door just as Mac was about to knock.

He grinned. "Elvis?"

I nodded.

"We made it," he said.

Jameis was beside him. He grinned and wrapped me in a bear hug. "I'm so glad to finally meet you for real," he said. He leaned back to look at me. "Man! You're even prettier in person."

I laughed. "And you're even taller in person."

"You know how they say good things come in little packages?" He held out his hands. "Well, sometimes they come in big packages."

Mac groaned. "I can't believe you're still using that line."

Jameis laughed. "You don't mess with perfection, big brother."

Jameis Mackenzie was Mac's height with the same dark hair and brown skin but he was heavier set with a beard and one pierced ear. He did have the same warm smile as his big brother.

"Do you have time for coffee and Rose's brownies?" I asked.

Mac looked at his brother. "It's up to you."

"Brownies?" he said. "Oh yes, we do have time."

Elvis was on top of the cat tower. He eyed Jameis with a bit of suspicion.

I went to start the coffee. Mac followed me and kissed the top of my head. "It is so, so good to see him."

"I like him," I said.

He smiled. "People always do."

We went back to the living room, where Jameis had already charmed Elvis, who was purring loudly as he got scratched behind his left ear.

"See what I mean?" Mac said.

Jameis turned to me. "Is it true you traded a junk car for this house?"

I laughed. "Not quite, but in a way yes."

Jameis sat on the sofa and patted the spot beside him. "This sounds like a story I need to hear."

"It's a long story, but basically I cleaned out a barn."

He frowned. "I'm not following."

"In the barn I found a Volkswagen Bug that hadn't been driven in at least twenty-five years. The woman who owned the barn said if I could get it out of there I could have it. So that's what I did."

"Good grief! How did you manage that?"

"I took the barn doors off and got six guys to pull it out. I was in college and guys at that age will pretty much do anything for beer."

He and Mac exchange a look, nodded and grinned.

"I did a little work on the car to get it running— well, I bribed my brother, Liam, to do a little work on the car." I smiled. "See previous reference to college guys and beer. I traded the bug for an old MG. The MG for a camper van, which my best friend, Jess, and I lived in for six months and which coincidentally is reason number one that I do not under any circumstances camp."

Jameis laughed.

"I traded the camper for a one-room cabin, where Jess and I lived for our last year of college, which is reason number two why I don't camp. I used the cabin as a down payment on this house."

I looked around. "It took a lot of work to get it to look this good and it wouldn't have happened without my dad and my brother."

"I'm impressed," Jameis said. He held up his thumb and index finger about half an inch apart.

"And just a little bit tired thinking about how much work it all was."

Mac came out of the kitchen with the coffee and the brownies.

"Oh man, are these good!" Jameis raved after he took his first bite. "Do you know what she puts in them? Do I taste a hint of instant espresso powder?"

"All I can tell you is that Rose is very particular about her cocoa," I said.

Jameis nodded. "So am I. A good Dutch-processed cocoa makes such a difference in flavor."

"I didn't know you were a baker," I said. I looked at Mac. "You didn't tell me."

He laughed. "That's because it's part of our misspent youth. Jameis has been baking since college."

I remembered Mac saying that when they were younger he and his brother weren't close, but that changed as they got older.

"Mac would do the main course and I would make dessert," Jameis said.

"Women love men who can cook," Mac said.

Jameis waggled his eyebrows. "Ain't that the truth."

"Well, you did win me over with your lasagna, and by the way I got some mozzarella at the farmers' market."

"Thank you," Mac said. "And I thought I won you over with my studly good looks." He struck a bodybuilder-type pose.

"No, I'm pretty sure it was the lasagna," I said.

Jameis almost choked on his coffee from laughing. We talked a bit about Jameis's work as a travel nurse and I noticed him try to stifle a yawn. "It's wonderful to have you here," I said, "but you should go get some rest and I'll see you in the morning."

"I am tired," he admitted, "but I promise it's not because of the company."

I gave Mac a hug. "How did things go at the market?" he asked.

"Well, at least we know Andrew has an alibi for Michael Norris's murder, so that's something. And we saw Simon there, which may or may not be something."

I hugged Jameis and we all said good night. He called good night to Elvis, who meowed back in response.

Rose was waiting in the hallway for me in the morning. She reached over and brushed something off my sweater. "You had brownies for breakfast," she said, her tone slightly accusatory.

"No, I didn't," I said. I sounded guilty. Not good.

Rose shook her head. "Then how did you get chocolate crumbs on your sweater?"

"It's all your fault," I said.

"And how did you come to that conclusion? I didn't come to your apartment and force-feed you brownies."

"You brought them to my apartment, which is the same thing, and it was *a* brownie, not brownies plural."

Rose tilted her head to one side and eyed me without speaking. I lasted about a minute.

"Okay. One and a half, which is not really brownies plural because it's not two."

"Your ability to rationalize is incredible."

I grinned. "Gram says the same thing."

As we went out to the car I told her that Jameis loved the brownies. "Do you add just a touch of instant espresso powder?"

Rose looks surprised. "I do," she said.

"Jameis thought so. He bakes."

"Wonderful," Rose said. "We can exchange recipes."

Jameis was waiting with Mac when they got to the shop. In no time he and Rose were talking about their spice cake recipes and alternatives to cream cheese frosting.

"Jameis just pulls people into his orbit wherever he goes," Mac said. "He's like our grandfather, our dad's dad."

"I really like your brother," I said, watching Jameis laugh at something Rose had just said, "but you're perfect just the way you are."

He leaned over and gave me a quick kiss on the cheek. "So tell me, really, it was my incredible good looks and charm that won you over, wasn't it?"

I shook my head. "Nope. It was really was the lasagna."

Rose decided to give everything in the shop a good dusting. Jameis went out to the workshop with Mac and I was about to go up to the office to get the website orders when Michelle walked in. She looked at Rose and then me and said, "Just who I was looking for."

"Is something wrong?"

She shook her head. "Surprisingly no, something is right. Some digging and a little surveillance revealed that the Glover sisters have been fencing stolen copper as well as catalytic converters. Their idea, apparently, of another type of recycling."

Rose gave me a smile.

"I knew it," I said. "Had Michael Norris figured it out?"

"We think he might have," Michelle said.

"Did Addie and Cherry have anything to do with his death?" Rose asked.

"No. They have an alibi. They were in the middle of, shall we say, a transaction, when Michael was killed."

"I know they've been breaking the law by dealing in stolen items," Rose said, "and that's not good, but I'm very glad they didn't kill anyone."

"The next time you two decide to go all *Law and Order*, how about calling me instead?" Michelle said.

"We just went to take a look at the street as part of our work for Josh Evans," Rose said.

Michelle almost seemed amused. "At midnight?"

"It was actually before midnight, but yes, it was late. Michael Norris was a night owl and he'd been having issues with his neighbors. It only made sense to drive by later in the evening to see what was going on."

Michelle looked a little chastened. "Fair point," she said.

"And it's *Cagney and Lacey*," I said.

She frowned. "Excuse me?"

"Not *Law and Order*, *Cagney and Lacey*."

She gave her head a little shake. "I'll try to remember that. Both of you try to stay on this side of the law."

Rose smiled. "We'll do our best."

Michelle left and I joined Rose. "How did you find out that Michael was a night owl?" I said.

"Oh, I'm just assuming he was," she said with a shrug.

"You lied," I said. "You lied to Michelle and you were good at it."

"I prefer the term 'embellished,' and yes, I am," she said. She raised one eyebrow. "You might want to remember that."

Chapter 22

Jess showed up at about nine thirty with several pillows she had made from an old quilt that I'd trash-picked. It had been worn thin in too many places to use for anything else.

"These are lovely," Rose said. "What do you think about putting them on the chair bench?"

"I like that idea," I said. "Hopefully they'll draw someone's attention."

"It's a fabulous piece of furniture," Jess said, running her hand lightly down one side of the dark wood.

"You could have the friends and family discount," Rose said with a smile.

Jess laughed. "Unfortunately I don't have a friends-and-family-size apartment."

Jameis and Mac came in and I introduced Jameis to Jess. "We should take you to the jam tonight," she said.

"What's the jam?" he asked.

"Only the best way to spend a Thursday night," Jess said. "Great food, live music and good company."

"They're going to see Mac's boat," I said.

"Actually we're going to look at a piece of spruce for the mast," Mac said.

"Come to the jam with us," Jess said. "It's more fun than a piece of wood."

I laughed. "Don't put him on the spot." Jess was not at all subtle. Probably why she and Liz got along so well.

Mac smiled. "It's up to you," he said to Jameis.

"Pick us! Pick us!" Jess chanted, pumping her arms in the air.

"This is hard," Jameis said.

"No, it's not. Pick us," Jess said.

Jameis looked at me.

I shook my head. "No way. I'm staying out of this."

He glanced down at Rose, raising his eyebrows.

She patted his arm. "You're a big boy. You can figure this out."

Mac laughed. "Oh, go with them. You know you want to."

Jameis held out his hands. "Ladies, I'm yours."

Jess and Rose started telling him what was on the menu at The Black Bear.

I walked over to Mac. "You don't mind?" I asked.

He smiled. "Are you sure you don't mind?"

I shook my head. "No. I want to spend more time with your brother. How else am I going to find out all the embarrassing stories about you?"

Jess left, Mac and Jameis went back out to the workshop and I finally went up to my office. Elvis was sitting in the middle of my desk. He reluctantly moved to one side to let me work.

I went back downstairs about half an hour later to find Nick in the shop looking at guitars while Rose showed a customer a pair of nightstands that were another trash-picked find.

I walked over to Nick and bumped him with my shoulder. "What are you doing here?"

"I have some news," he said. "Josh likely knows by now, but I wanted to tell you all myself. It was my assignment, after all."

"What is it?" I said.

"The medical examiner's final report is done."

"And?"

"Michael Norris didn't die from anaphylaxis."

I stared at him and I'm pretty sure my mouth fell open just a little.

"Did you notice anything about the body?" Nick asked.

The image of Michael Norris's body lying on the sand as I pulled the seaweed away from his face was something I was trying not to think about. I took a slow breath and tried to remember every detail I'd seen. "He had an injury to the back of his head. I assumed he'd hit it on something when he went into the water."

"There was no water in his lungs," Nick said.

"But . . . but that means he was dead when he went in the water."

He nodded.

"So he didn't go into anaphylaxis, then fall into the water and hit his head."

"No, he didn't. He did have a reaction to the hummus that would have disabled him enough for it to be easy for whoever killed him to hit him over the head. After that it looks as though the killer left the body on the beach where the incoming tide pulled it out."

I closed my eyes for a moment. I could taste something sour at the back of my throat.

"Are you all right?" Nick asked.

I opened my eyes. "I'm okay," I said. "I just wasn't expecting this."

"Yeah, well, for what it's worth I don't think anyone was." He glanced at his watch. "I have to get going."

"Thanks for coming," I said. "I'll tell everyone else."

"One more thing. Since it looks like Michael and his killer were on the beach and not on the breakwater the evidence suggests the person who hit Michael was about average height. And I didn't tell you that."

I nodded. "Okay."

He seemed to be waiting for me to say something else. "What?" I asked.

"Glenn is tall."

I realized what he meant. Glenn couldn't have killed Michael.

I felt my shoulders sag with relief. "Glenn is in the clear."

"Not one hundred percent but he looks less and less like a viable suspect."

I threw my arms around him. "I'll take it. Best news I've had all week."

"Yeah, me too," he said.

"Will we see you tonight?" I asked.

"As far as I know. Save me a seat."

I promised I would and he left.

Rose came over to ask if I could help carry out the nightstands.

"Of course," I said.

"What was Nicolas doing here?" she asked.

"He had some news. I'll tell you in a minute."

Rose rang up the customer and he and I carried out the nightstands and got them settled on the backseat of his car.

"You have a lot of great things in your shop," he said. "I'll definitely be back."

"Thank you," I said. "I hope we see you again."

I went back inside and told Rose what Nick said. "Glenn is still a suspect but he's not at the top of the list anymore."

"That's wonderful news," she said. "Is Nick certain about the cause of death?"

"I think the medical examiner knows what he's doing," I said.

"Oh heavens, I didn't mean to suggest he doesn't," Rose said. "It's just that I thought anaphylaxis could kill a person."

"Not always," Jameis said. He was standing behind us. We both turned to look at him.

"Sorry," he said. "I didn't mean to eavesdrop. You're right that anaphylaxis can kill a person but anaphylaxis itself isn't that common. And when it does happen deaths are rare."

"I had no idea," Rose said.

Jameis shrugged. "Most people don't." He held up two mugs. "Where do I find more coffee?"

Rose smiled. "I'll show you."

I spent most of the morning in the store with Rose. We had a steady stream of customers. Jon Everly stopped in to say my proposal for cleaning out his aunt's house worked for him and his mother and he'd like to hire us. We discussed possible dates and settled on getting started in three weeks.

When Avery arrived at about eleven o'clock Greg was with her. I was at the workbench looking for some more maps for her to frame. We had sold two more of the old photos and I needed something for the bare spaces on the wall. Out of the corner of my eye I saw Avery gives Greg a nudge and he walked over to me.

"Hi, Greg," I said.

He was tall and lanky with dark brown hair and dark eyes. He always seemed a little guarded but he'd spent enough time with all of us that he was beginning to relax.

"Avery said you might have some extra work this summer," he said.

"I do," I said, putting down the map I'd been examining. "It's dirty, tedious work cleaning out someone's house."

"I know how to work hard," he said. "I'm not lazy."

I explained some of what was involved. "It's important to respect the privacy of the people whose home we're in, so no taking photos of anything and posting them online and no gossiping about the house or its contents with your friends."

"I would never do that," he said. "People gossiped about my family. I know how crappy that feels." Greg's father had been involved in one of the Angels' former cases.

"Great," I said. "You're hired."

Greg smiled and to my surprise held out his hand. We shook hands and he thanked me. He turned to go join Avery, who had gone into the shop, probably to give us a little privacy, and then turned back around. "Avery told you about that guy at the sandwich shop who was arguing with Glenn, right?"

I nodded. "She did."

"Okay, good," he said. "Did anyone tell you about the other guy? He had to have seen everything as well, and he was outside so he probably heard the argument. I'm not sure Avery even saw him because she went to get a muffin to take to school and it takes her forever to pick what she wants."

"Hang on a minute," I said. "What other guy?"

Greg suddenly looked uncomfortable. "This guy was coming up the street and when Glenn and the man started getting loud he stopped and stepped behind that big elm tree just before the corner."

I nodded to encourage him to keep going.

"The guy was mostly behind the tree and I was trying not to look like I was watching him, so I didn't get a real good look, but he had dark hair, he wasn't really heavy and he had a messenger bag over one shoulder. I've seen him at the market a few times."

That wasn't much to go on. "That's it?" I said.

"Yeah, I think so," he said. Then he hesitated. "Oh yeah, he looked Asian."

"Are you certain?" I asked.

Greg nodded. "I'm positive. I could see him well enough to know that."

"And there's nothing else?"

"No," he said.

"Thanks for telling me."

I waited until Greg had gone into the store and then went to the Angels' office. Mr. P. was on the phone. I paced outside the door until he got off the call.

He looked and smiled at me. "Did you need something, Sarah?" he asked.

"Simon Kang lied to Liz and me," I said.

"I thought we had already established that he must have been lying about something given how fidgety he seemed."

I felt a little fidgety myself. "He knew that Michael had seen something the night of Freddie Black's murder and kept it to himself. He was at the sandwich shop. Greg saw him. Simon heard Glenn and Michael arguing. He told Liz and me that Andrew would have had no reason to want to kill Michael but he did. Michael might have been able to keep him from going to prison. Simon knew that."

"Maybe his loyalty to Andrew Lewis runs deeper than we thought," Mr. P. said. "That would explain why he didn't say anything. It does, however, make his loyalty to Glenn a little suspect."

"That's what I thought," I said.

Mr. P. tapped the notepad to the right of his computer. "I have found out a little more about Simon. I've learned some of what happened in front of the grand jury even though the transcripts are not public documents here in Maine."

"Were any laws broken?"

He smiled. "You know I try to be a law-abiding citizen, and as I told you before, witnesses can talk about what happened. There are no restrictions on them. No one else can do that. I feel confident that Simon Kang was one of the witnesses who testified in front of the grand jury. I believe that Elyse Tremblay, the young woman who we learned died in a car accident in Australia, was the other witness."

I nodded.

"I have an idea, call it a hunch, that I need to check out."

"Would you like to share with the class?" I asked.

Mr. P. smiled. "I'm not at the sharing stage yet, but when I am you'll be one of the first to know."

I was up in my office about twenty minutes later, making a list of items I wanted Avery to add to the website, when my brother, Liam, called.

"Hey, are you interested in some vintage Bachman model train sets?" he asked.

When he told me the price I said yes. "Grab them for me, please," I said. "I'll send you the money."

"And I have some chairs for you that came out of an old store I'm involved in renovating. I saved them from going to the landfill."

"Why would someone want to put chairs in the landfill?" I said. "I've put chairs back together that were in pieces. It's such a waste."

Liam laughed. "You are so weird about chairs," he said. "I'm hoping to be there by the end of next week to spend some time looking over Michelle's house, so I'll bring them for you then."

"The real estate market is pretty good right now," I said. "Hint, hint."

"Yeah, I wanted to talk to you about that. I have decided to move closer but I'm not moving to North Harbor."

My heart sank. I had been lobbying for Liam to put down roots here for a while. I wanted to spend more time with him.

"But I am moving closer to Mom and Dad so you will see me more often. I have an eye on a couple of houses."

It was better than him saying he was moving to the other end of the country.

"Send me pictures of both of them," I said. "I'd love to have you in North Harbor, but I like the idea that you'll be a little closer and you'd better visit more often."

He laughed. "If you see me too often you might not appreciate my charming personality as much."

I laughed as well. "Good point."

"I gotta go," he said. "Love you, *baby* sister." He put extra emphasis on the word "baby."

Liam and I were not biological siblings. My mom and his dad had gotten married when we were kids but the biology didn't matter to us. Liam was just a few months older and he loved to remind me of that.

"Love you, too, old man," I said.

I ended the call and looked at Elvis, who had come

over and jumped on my desk halfway through the call. "Liam isn't moving to North Harbor," I said.

The cat wrinkled his nose and made a sound a lot like a sigh.

I nodded. "That's how I feel, too."

Mr. P. poked his head around the half-open door. "I'm calling Emily Young again. Would you like to join the call?"

"Your hunch?"

"Yes," he said. "I'm trying to place everyone at the time Freddie went into the water and I'm not having much luck. Emily talked about being with some young man and I'm wondering who it was."

I nodded.

"I'd like to find out if she can remember his name. There's no point in going off on what might be a wild-goose chase."

We headed down to his office, trailed by Elvis, and made the video call to Emily. She waved at the screen.

"How do you feel?" I asked.

"Like a balloon ready to pop any moment." She patted her belly and smiled.

"I'm wondering if you've been able to remember the name of the young man you . . ." Mr. P. hesitated.

"Made out with," Emily said. "It's okay. I'm not offended by the words. I've been trying to remember and all I keep coming up with is the Chipmunks."

"You mean the cartoon characters who did the Christmas song?" I said. I could suddenly hear my heart thumping in my ears.

She nodded. "That's the ones. Could his name have been Alvin?"

"What about Simon?" I said.

She smiled. "Yes. It was Simon."

Mr. P. and I exchanged a look that Emily noticed.

"Is that bad?" she asked.

I shook my head. "No, it isn't."

Mr. P. thanked her for her help.

"We'd love to see a photo when the baby gets here," I added.

Emily promised she'd send one and we said good-bye.

"Well, I wasn't expecting that," Mr. P. said.

I stared up at the ceiling as if I could find answers to the questions spinning in my head. There weren't any. "Could Simon have seen Freddie and Andrew arguing if he was drunk and making out with Emily?" I asked.

Mr. P. raised one eyebrow. "Interesting question. I think we need to find out."

Chapter 23

"We need to talk to Simon again," I said. An idea had burrowed into the back of my brain. I wasn't sure I was ready to share it yet.

"Agreed," Mr. P. said, "but he has no reason to talk to us."

"We could tell Michelle what we know."

"It may come to that, but it's almost lunchtime. Perhaps we could drive over to the school and see if Mr. Kang goes out for lunch."

I bumped him with my elbow. "The old-ambush-'em-in-the-parking-lot ploy."

He smiled. "And we always have send-Elizabeth-to-talk-to-him-again as a backup plan."

We got to the school just before noon. Since it was exam week and exams seemed to be over for the day, there weren't a lot of cars around. I pointed at the silver Audi I'd noticed the last time.

"I think that might be Simon's car," I said to Mr. P.

just as it pulled out of its parking spot with Simon behind the wheel.

On impulse I followed.

"Keep an eye on the car," I said. Simon drove aggressively and I didn't want to lose him, but I didn't want to give us away, either.

"In my admittedly limited experience people don't expect to be tailed on a Thursday in North Harbor, Maine," he said, "but I will do my best."

We followed Simon to The Black Bear. Mr. P. and I waved a hello to Sam, who was at the bar when we walked in. Simon was at a booth, looking at the menu. We went over to him.

"The spicy chicken burger is good," I said.

He looked up at me and frowned. "You're Mrs. French's assistant," he said.

"And I'm Alfred Peterson," Mr. P. said. "I'm a private investigator working for a local attorney." He offered Josh's card.

"Mrs. French is determined," Simon said. He laid the card on the table.

It seemed he assumed that Liz had hired Josh. I had no intention of correcting that assumption. If Liz's name helped us I had no problem with that.

"What do you want?" he asked.

"You lied," I said. "You knew that Andrew Lewis was out of jail."

I saw a flash of surprise on Mr. P.'s face but he covered it well.

Simon flushed. "That doesn't change anything. Andrew wouldn't have jeopardized his freedom by killing Michael."

"Even if he knew that Michael might have been able to have kept him from going to jail in the first place?" Mr. P. said.

Simon stared down at the table.

"We know that you heard Michael and Glenn arguing," Mr. P. said.

I tapped the top of the table with a finger and channeled Liz. "Two people are dead. It's time to start telling the truth."

"The person Michael saw arguing with Freddie was me. My father was paying for college and I'd already failed a class. If I had failed another one he had warned me that he'd stop paying for my living expenses. So I might have gotten a little help on an essay, and Freddie kind of found out about it."

"In other words you paid someone to write an essay for you and Freddie was going to turn you in," I said.

He finally looked up at me, anger pulling at the lines around his mouth. "It was none of her business. All she had to do was keep her mouth shut. I would have made it worth her while." He looked like a petulant child.

"You made the mistake of trying to buy her silence," Mr. P. said. It seemed to me I could hear a hint of disapproval in his voice.

"It wasn't like that," Simon snapped. "I just wanted her to keep quiet and in return I was willing to help her out with a couple of expenses. That's all."

"How did you get Michael to keep what he saw to himself?" I asked. I was feeling my way, trying to ask the questions that might help us figure out what really happened all those years ago.

Simon gave a snort. "First of all Michael wasn't all righteous about not taking any money for helping out a friend."

"Michael didn't need money," Mr. P. said.

"Yes, he did. His parents were paying for his tuition but Michael was paying for his books and expenses and he'd lost his scholarship at the end of the year because his grades were down. He didn't want his parents to know."

I glanced at Mr. P. This wasn't what I'd expected. Simon seemed to be totally without remorse.

"So Michael was willing to let his friend go to jail for money," Mr. P. said.

Simon shrugged. "When it comes down to it, self-interest will pretty much always win out. Plus Michael had been drinking a lot that night. He'd already been picked up once before for DUI and he was afraid his parents would cut the money off entirely if they found out he was still drinking. I managed to convince Michael that I had seen Andrew and Freddie arguing and it was likely Andrew who was responsible for her death."

"But you didn't see them. Did you?" I said. "You were too busy making out with Emily Young. You lied to the grand jury. You lied to everyone."

Simon closed his eyes for a moment. When he opened them again I saw the first sign of regret on his face. "You have to understand I was a dumb kid at the time." His voice dropped to just above a whisper. "And I thought it was possible that I might actually have pushed her. Then one of the girls said she saw

Freddie arguing with Andrew and I just confirmed the story to draw attention away from myself."

"What's wrong with you?" I said. "You might have put an innocent person in jail because you were drunk and stupid."

Mr. P. put a hand on my arm and gave it a squeeze. "Take a breath, Sarah," he said in a low voice.

My hands were shaking.

"I know I did the wrong thing," Simon said. "Andrew always insisted he was innocent and when I heard Michael and Glenn arguing I thought this could be a chance to maybe fix what I'd done."

"You had the last fourteen-plus years to fix what you'd done by telling the truth," Mr. P. said.

"Where were you was the day Michael was killed? The truth," I said. I put my hands in my pockets, both of them clenched into tight fists to try to stop the trembling.

Simon shook his head. "I didn't hurt Michael. He was my chance to redeem myself."

Simon Kang was one of the most self-absorbed people I'd ever met.

"I was out with some friends when Michael died. I hadn't decided what I was going to do," he said, "and I'm not pulling them into this, so don't ask for their names." That glimpse of regret I'd thought I'd seen on his face was gone. "And I'm done talking to you."

I opened my mouth to say something and Mr. P. gave my arm another squeeze. "Time for us to go," he said quietly.

Simon was looking at the menu again. I had the

urge to pull it out of his hands and smack him over the head with it. It wouldn't have accomplished anything, but I was certain it would have made me feel better.

Mr. P. and I walked back to the car in silence. Once I had fastened my seat belt I turned to look at him. "Thank you for not letting me do something stupid back there," I said.

"I understand the impulse," he said with a smile. "And I don't actually think you would have given in to it."

"I'm not so sure," I said. "Simon Kang is so unbelievably self-absorbed."

Mr. P. fastened his seat belt and smoothed down his few whips of gray hair. "He certainly is," he said. "Not a good way to go through life."

I started the SUV and pulled out of our parking spot.

"How did you know Simon knew Andrew Lewis was out of jail?" Mr. P. asked as we started back to Second Chance. "I missed that entirely."

"A fair amount of luck," I said, "and Greg."

"Avery's Greg?" he said. "I'm afraid I'm going to need a little more detail."

"When he described the man he saw I figured out it had to be Simon because of the physical description."

Mr. P. nodded.

"I was so focused on the physical description that I almost let something else Greg said slip by me."

"That doesn't sound like you, my dear. What was it?"

"Greg said he thought he had seen the man at the market a few times," I said.

Out of the corner of my eye I saw his expression change as he made the connection I'd made. "We saw Simon at the farmers' market as well," he said.

"And if he was a regular, which it sounds like he was . . ." I began.

"Then he would have known Andrew was out of prison because he would have seen him at the Pine Knoll Farm stall," Mr. P. finished. "Excellent deductive reasoning."

It was another piece to the puzzle but, once again, I had idea what to do with it.

"Do you think Simon killed Michael Norris?" I asked Mr. P.

"You know, I don't," he said. "It seems that would have taken more effort than he would put in."

"I agree with you," I said, "but I feel like we're running out of suspects."

Mr. P. nodded. "I'd like to disagree with you, but at the moment, I can't."

Jameis came with Rose, Mr. P., Elvis and me at the end of the day. He sat on the sofa with Elvis on his lap while I got ready.

"You know, Mac seems happy, really happy with all of you and I'm glad to see that."

"He's opened up a lot in the last year," I said.

"Your friends are terrific," Jameis said. "It's scary what Mr. P. can do with a computer and I wish I'd had teachers like Rose and Charlotte when I was in school."

"They wrapped Mom and Gram and me in love when my father died and I wouldn't be who I am now without them. And they know every dumb, embarrassing thing I've ever done and love me anyway." I came out of the bedroom carrying my jacket because it was supposed to rain.

Jameis grinned. "So I heard."

I groaned. "And they love to share every dumb and embarrassing thing I've ever done."

"Is it true you blew up the kitchen in your home ec class?" he asked.

"I did not blow up the kitchen," I said with a little more indignation than I had intended. "There may have been a small fire, but that's all. They only sent one fire truck."

Jameis laughed.

Jess was already at the pub and had grabbed us a table. We all ordered supper. Jess and I pushed Jameis to try Sam's bacon burger on a homemade sourdough bun. He swooned when he tasted it.

Nick arrived just before Sam and the guys got started. I introduced him to Jameis and they shook hands.

The band was on fire. Jameis grabbed Jess by the hand and they danced and laughed, moving together like they'd been dancing with each other for a long time.

"Mac's brother is a bit of a flirt," Nick whispered.

"You jealous?" I teased.

"No," he said, a little too quickly.

"Jess is a big girl and she can handle herself."

"I know," he said but he continued to watch them closely.

In the break Nick excused himself to speak to someone. Jess was turned around talking to someone at the next table.

Jameis propped an elbow on the table and leaned toward me. "Hey, is there anything between Jess and Nick?" he asked.

"Jess and Nick? No," I said. Then I thought about how Nick had almost seemed jealous when Jameis and Jess were dancing. "No," I repeated with a bit less certainty.

"Have you ever noticed that sometimes you take a person or a thing for granted and it takes someone else's interest to make you notice what was right in front of you all along?" Jameis said. He smiled. "I'm just saying."

Glenn came over then. "Sarah, do you have a minute?" he asked.

"Go," Jameis said. "I'm good."

We stepped away from the table. "I talked to Josh before I left," Glenn said. "The police no longer see me as a suspect." He smiled.

I smiled back at him. "No one who knows you ever thought you were," I said.

"Please keep going," he said. "No matter what Michael did or didn't do, we were friends at one time. Good friends. Please, find out what happened."

"All right," I said, knowing the others would agree.

The second set was as good as the first and when the guys were finally done Jameis thanked Jess and me for bringing him. "I had so much fun." Then he turned to Nick. "Thanks for letting me crash your Thursday night. I appreciate it."

"Glad you came," Nick said.

I was about to offer Jess a ride home when Nick beat me to it.

"This is getting to be a habit," she said, "but yes, I'll take the drive."

Jameis gave her a hug.

"I hope I see you again before you leave," she said.

He smiled. "Count on it."

I drove Jameis back to Mac's apartment.

"How did you come to open Second Chance?" he said.

I explained how I had come to sulk at my grandmother's house after I'd lost my radio job, and how that had turned into this.

"In other words you went after what you wanted."

I laughed. "Yeah, I guess I kind of did. So did Mac, by coming to North Harbor."

Mac was waiting by the apartment door.

"Did you get the wood for the mast?" I asked.

He smiled. "I did." He looked at his brother. "So? Did you have a good time?"

"Are you kidding?" Jameis said. "It was fantastic." He leaned over and gave me a one-armed hug. "Thanks for inviting me."

"I'm glad you came with us," I said. "It was a lot of fun." I glanced at Mac. "And I'm going to get going. It's been a busy day."

"Sarah, could you stay for a moment?" Jameis asked.

"There's something I want to talk to Mac—and you—about."

"Okay," I said. I looked at Mac, who frowned and gave his head a little shake. It seemed he didn't know what Jameis wanted to talk about.

We went inside. I took a seat on the sofa and Mac sat on the arm.

"I'm not going to waste your time with a lot of preamble," Jameis said. He looked nervous, rubbing the palms of his hands together. "Mac, I want to sell Mom's piano. I don't know if you remember the Morrisons who used to live next door to us, but Kamela Morrison wants to buy it. I want to use my share to help pay for medical school." He couldn't help smiling.

"You're going to medical school?" I said.

He nodded. "I've been accepted into the Long School of Medicine in San Antonio. Between scholarships, what I've saved and my share of the money from the piano, I should be able to graduate pretty much debt-free."

"That's wonderful news," I said.

I glanced at Mac. He was smiling. "Sarah's right. It is wonderful news," he said. "I'm proud of you."

"But," Jameis said.

"I don't see why we have to sell Mom's piano for you to go."

I knew Mac had a strong, sentimental attachment to the piano, a custom Steinway that had belonged to his grandmother and then his mother.

"C'mon, Mac," Jameis said. "That piano has been in

storage for years. It's such a waste. Neither one of us can even play it."

I recognized that stubborn, closed-off look on Mac's face. "I don't understand why you even want to sell it," he said. "You can borrow the rest of what you need for medical school and easily pay it back when you graduate."

Jameis was already shaking his head. "The kind of doctor I want to be doesn't make a lot of money. I want to practice in a rural area and take care of people who can't afford and don't have access to good medical care. I want to work with the kind of communities I have been working with for the past four years. And in case you've forgotten Mom would understand that."

"Why didn't you tell me you were applying to medical schools?" Mac asked. "I could have helped."

Jameis pulled one hand across the back of his neck. "Because I wanted to do this without my big brother's help. Can you understand that?"

"No, I can't," Mac said, anger sharpening his voice. "Why would you want to leave me out of such a momentous change in your life? Why am I only hearing about all of this now?"

"I understand," I said.

They both looked at me.

I cleared my throat. "When I was house-hunting I didn't tell Liam—or anyone else, for that matter—until I found the house I wanted. I needed to prove to myself that I could manage my life on my own terms."

I gave Mac's leg a squeeze and turned my attention to Jameis. "But I can also understand how it hurts

Mac that you kept such a big secret, because Liam just made a choice about where he's going to live and he didn't talk to me about the decision until he'd made it."

"I'll loan you the money for medical school, but I won't agree to sell our mother's piano," Mac said. "It's true neither of us play, but someday one or both of us could have a child that will."

"I'm not taking your money," Jameis said. "You don't make that kind of money anymore, which means you'll have to borrow it or take it out of your retirement account. You're not going in debt for me to go to school. And I don't want to be rescued by my big brother. I'm not six anymore."

"I know that," Mac said.

"Then start treating me like an adult," Jameis retorted, "and start acting like one yourself. What will we do if we both have children who love music the way Mom did? Will we cut the piano in half? Wheel it back and forth between our houses? It's a thing, Mac. And Mom would want to see it played and loved and not have it come between the two of us." He threw up his hands and shook his head. "I can't talk to you," he said and then he walked out.

The silence hung in the room like it was a wall between Mac and his brother.

"Am I wrong?" Mac finally said.

"I get how you feel," I said, choosing my words carefully. "I understand that connection you have to your mother through her piano. But based on what you've told me about her, I also think that Jameis has a point. Your mother would have wanted the piano to be played and enjoyed."

"You don't play your father's guitar," he said, finally looking at me. "How is that different?"

His words felt like a slap.

"You're right, I don't," I said. I stood up and faced him. "And that's a completely different situation. Jameis wants to be a doctor. He wants to help people. I've only spent one day with your brother and I know he'll make that happen. But you can make the whole thing easier for him. I think you're wrong and I think maybe I've been wrong about things, too." And then I left as well.

When I got home I got the guitar out of the closet. It was very out of tune and my fingers felt the same way. I had a lot of memories of Dad playing that guitar. They were both happy and sad reminders of him. And there weren't nearly enough of them.

I thought about what Jameis had said, that his mother would want her piano to be played. I knew Dad would feel the same way about his guitar, especially because it had been lost to me for so long. Finally I took a deep breath and began to tune the strings.

Chapter 24

The next morning I got up early and went for a long run. By chance I met up with Caroline Vega, an artist friend, and we ran together and caught up on each other's lives. As we were making a loop around the park I spotted Joanna Norris waiting to cross the street, carrying what looked to be a stainless-steel coffee mug. I waved hello and Joanna waved back, crossed and went to the coffee shop on the corner. I wondered if anyone was ever going to be able to give Joanna answers about her brother's death.

When I got home Mac was sitting in front of my door. He looked as though he hadn't gotten much sleep. There were lines around his eyes and he hadn't shaved. He had a box from Glenn's bakery balanced on one knee. He stood up and brushed off his pants. "I'm so sorry," he said. He handed me the box.

I looked inside to find half a dozen blueberry muffins with the crackle tops I loved. "Where did you get these?" I asked.

"I called Glenn very early, told him I had screwed up big-time and begged him to help me."

"Come in," I said.

Mac stood in the middle of my living room, looking more serious than I'd ever seen him. "You're not wrong about us. I know I messed up, but you and I are really good together."

I held up one hand. "Stop right there. When did I say I thought I was wrong about us? I'm pretty sure I'd remember that."

"You said it last night. You told me I was wrong about Jameis and then you said you thought you'd been wrong about things, too."

"About my dad's guitar, not about us. You were right about the guitar. And I can't tell you what to do with respect to Jameis and the piano, but I can tell you that I'm not leaving my dad's guitar in the closet any longer." I held out my left hand so he could see the reddened ends of my fingers from where I'd played the night before.

"We're okay," he said. There was a hint of uncertainty in his voice.

"It would take more than your mother's piano to come between us," I said. "In fact I don't know what it would take."

Mac smiled. "I had a speech I was going to give you about how good we are for each other."

I smiled back at him. "I'd love to hear it." I tipped my head in the direction of the kitchen. "Could I just make coffee first?"

He caught my hand and pressed a kiss into my

palm. "I'm sorry I acted the way I did about the piano. I have all these wonderful memories of my mother playing and singing for Jameis and me." He ducked his head for a moment. "And those memories won't change, no matter who owns it."

"They won't," I said.

Mac took a breath and let it out slowly. "Last night when Jameis came back I told him two things. One, that I am so proud of him for getting into medical school, and two, to take the offer for the piano. And now I have two things to say to you. One is that I was horrible about your father's guitar and I'm truly sorry for hurting you. If you don't want to play it, you don't have to."

I smiled. "I do want to play it. And what's the second thing?"

He was still holding my hand and now he pulled me toward him. "I love you," he said.

It was the first time he'd ever said the words to me. I grinned at him and threw my arms around his neck feeling a rush of happiness. "I love you, too," I said.

I was in my office just after we opened, making a list of the website orders, when Mr. P. and Rose tapped on my door. "C'mon in," I called.

Mr. P. had what I called his cat-that-swallowed-the-canary look on his face.

"I know that look," I said. "What did you find?"

He turned the computer around. "Take a look for yourself," Rose said.

It was security video of Simon Kang passed out in

his car. Based on the light it looked to be late afternoon. "That's the day Michael Norris was killed, isn't it?" I said.

"Yes, it is," she said.

"How did you find that?" I looked from the laptop screen to the two of them and back again.

"The Black Bear has a lot of loyal customers," Mr. P. said. "It occurred to me that maybe Simon was one of them. I talked to Sammy and a couple of the bartenders and one of them remembered him. He'd had too much to drink and they cut him off. After that all I had to do was look for security footage from some of the businesses in the area. As you can see, he isn't our killer."

"Then who is?" I said in frustration. "Every lead we've followed has ended up as a dead end. Andrew Lewis has an alibi. No one ever thought it was Glenn. Simon was drunk and passed out in his car. None of the other people who were there the night that Freddie Black died could have killed Michael and we still don't know what the heck he was doing out there on that stretch of beach in the first place."

"We'll figure it out," Mr. P. said.

I made a strangled sound of frustration. "Will we? There could be someone out there who got away with Freddie Black's murder and now they're going to get away with another one."

"Go take some time off," Rose said. "We can take care of things here."

I raked a hand back through my hair. "I can't. I have things to do."

"Nothing that won't wait," she said firmly. "Let the

world turn without you for a while." She looked at me and frowned slightly as though she was sizing me up. Then she turned to Mr. P. "If you take her arms, I can take her feet."

"Fine," I said. "I'm going. You don't have to carry me out." I stopped to plant a kiss on the top of her head, then I grabbed my bag and headed downstairs.

I got in the car and drove out of the parking lot with no particular destination in mind. I had been more affected by Michael Norris's death than I'd realized. I remembered how cold his skin had felt when Glenn and I dragged his body out of the water. I remembered pulling the seaweed away from his face and discovering that piece of old tarp twisted around his head. I hadn't known him at all, but his death still hurt.

I found myself headed in the direction of the beach and decided to keep going. I glanced in the rearview mirror. The same small, black car had been behind me since I'd left Second Chance. Was someone following me? I slowed down. So did the black car. I sped up a little. The driver behind me did the same. He or she wasn't very good at surveillance. I looked for somewhere to turn around and head back to the shop. I glanced in the rearview mirror again just in time to see the little car pull into a driveway.

I blew out a breath. I wasn't being followed. My brain was just overloaded. Whoever had been behind me had just been headed in the same direction and trying to stay in the flow of traffic. I decided I'd head to the water after all.

When I got there I parked in front of Mac's garage.

There was no sign of Memphis's SUV. I walked down to the beach and the sound of the water slowly eased my frustration. I went out onto the breakwater where Freddie Black had died and wondered if we'd been wrong all this time. Maybe Freddie's death had nothing to do with Michael's. Maybe the fact that Michael died on this same stretch of beach really was just a coincidence.

Except I couldn't convince myself that was true. What had Michael been doing out here? We still had no idea. I picked up a small, flat rock and sent it skipping across the water—one, two, three. It occurred to me that maybe I was asking the wrong question. Maybe what I needed to figure out was who could have gotten Michael out to that stretch of beach. Why would I come to a place that held horrible memories for me? I'd do it for Mac. Or for Rose or Mr. P. I'd set my feelings aside for my grandmother or Liam or Mom and Dad. I would show up somewhere that made my skin crawl for pretty much anyone I loved. And I knew I was lucky that was a long list.

I thought about Michael. He didn't have a lot of people in his life. The person he cared about was Joanna. She'd said herself that he was a good big brother. The breeze tugged at my hair and I tucked a strand behind one ear.

Things still didn't make sense. Why would Joanna have killed her brother? I remembered her telling me how she would do anything to fix the mess Michael had left behind. I could hear the intensity in her voice when she said he was the most important person in the world to her. She'd seemed embarrassed by her outburst. That was why I'd told her I understood because I had a brother as well.

I felt a shiver, like something had just crawled across the back of my neck. What if Joanna wasn't talking about her brother when she got so emotional? In the context of what she'd been saying it could just as easily have been Andrew Lewis. And just like that I realized that this was the missing piece that made all the other pieces of the puzzle fit together. Joanna was in love with Andrew. It was enough of a motive for her to have killed her brother.

I needed to head back and explain what I'd figured out to Rose and Mr. P. We needed to dig a little deeper into Joanna's life to see if we could find some proof. I turned from the water to find Joanna Norris standing on the sand.

"Hi," I said. "What are you doing here?"

"Probably the same thing you're doing, trying to find a way to make things work out."

I felt a bit uncomfortable with how intently Joanna was watching me. I took a couple of steps toward the sand and Joanna came a little closer.

"I talked to Glenn," she said. "He told me that he asked you and your friends to keep trying to figure out who killed my brother. I wanted to tell you that you don't need to do that. Now that Glenn's name is cleared, the police will do the rest. I would have told you this morning, but you had someone with you."

There was something unsettling about her smile. It was a bit too cheery and it never seemed to falter.

My stomach clenched. "Are you following me?" I

asked. Had I been right about that little black car? Had that been Joanna?

"Like I said, I couldn't talk to you this morning." She took another step toward me and I wondered why she was keeping one hand behind her back.

"Well, I'm glad you found me. Let's go somewhere and have a cup of coffee and figure out what our next steps should be."

Joanna shook her head. "There's no need to do that. I already told you. Let the police do their job. In the end, Michael was responsible for his own death."

I felt a shiver slide down my spine.

She took another step toward me and climbed up on the breakwater so we were only a few feet apart.

I shook my head. "I'm sorry. I don't understand." But I was afraid that maybe I did. "Joanna, what are you holding behind your back?" I asked.

"Nothing," she said, but her gaze slipped away from mine for a moment.

"Then show me, please."

Joanna sighed and held out her hand. She was holding a large rock. She must have picked it up on the beach. "I'm sorry, Sarah," she said. "I didn't want to scare you."

"Please put that down," I said.

"I'm sorry, I can't because I might need it."

My heart was pounding so hard I was surprised she couldn't hear it. "Are you going to hurt me?"

She shook her head. "No. You're a reasonable person and we can work this out." She sighed. "My brother was not reasonable."

"You killed him," I said, working to keep my voice steady and gentle.

Joanna pushed her hair back off her face. "No. I already told you that Michael was responsible for what happened to him."

"I don't understand. What did he do?"

For the first time Joanna seemed annoyed. "He did nothing, don't you see that?"

"You mean he didn't tell anyone about seeing Freddie fight with someone other than Andrew."

"How could he do that to his friend? How could he do that to his own sister?"

I saw the gleam of tears in her eyes and it was impossible to miss the pain in her voice. I was right. Joanna Norris had been in love with Andrew Lewis. Still was.

"You were in love with Andrew," I said.

Joanna nodded. "I had no idea Michael had information that would have helped Andrew. When I found out I told him he had to tell Andrew and his lawyer and the police. There had to be a way to get the case reopened because it wasn't like a jury had convicted him, so there had to be a way to undo it all. Michael said it wasn't that easy."

I looked around, trying to figure out how to make my way around Joanna, but the tide was coming in rapidly and I was afraid I might fall on the rocks if I tried to jump to one side.

"Freddie and I were friends. Freddie was like a big sister. And I love Andrew. Michael knew that."

I noticed she'd said "love." Present tense.

"I couldn't breathe when I found out that he'd been keeping this secret for all these years," Joanna said, and I could hear the pain in her voice. "I confronted him and he admitted it. Freddie's real killer might have been walking around for the last fifteen years. And all that time I could have been with Andrew was gone."

"I'm so sorry," I said. I took one small step forward and hoped she didn't notice.

"Andrew ended our relationship when he was arrested. He said I had to keep it to myself so people wouldn't judge me. I told him I didn't want to but he said he needed me to do it for him. And now that he's out of prison, he loves me so much he won't get back together because he still thinks I'll be stigmatized. I told him I don't care but he said he could never do that to me."

"You must have been so angry," I said. "I would have been. I don't know what I would have done. What did you do?" Maybe if I could keep her talking I could make my way off the rocks.

"I convinced Michael to meet me here. He was just trying to placate me but I thought once I got him out here he'd reconsider."

"Reconsider what? Michael had already talked to Glenn and Glenn had told him he had to come clean."

Joanna was already shaking her head. "He wasn't going to. Don't you get it? My brother was a coward. He wasn't going to talk to the police or the prosecutor or Andrew's lawyer. He wasn't going to tell the truth. He was going to say he had been drinking and Glenn had misunderstood the whole conversation."

She was breathing hard, fury flashing in her eyes.

"You brought the food," I said. "The hummus. The soft pretzels. You wanted to hurt him."

"I told Michael I was hungry. I asked him to come sit with me and maybe we could figure out a way to fix things without him having to admit he lied."

"But why did you put the tahini in that container of hummus?" I asked.

She sighed. "I wouldn't have used it if Michael had just listened to reason. I just wanted to scare him. I wanted him to say what he'd done out loud and then I could record him with my phone. But he wouldn't say it. He kept saying Andrew was back to his life and everything was all right and I had to let it be. I knew a bit of hummus wouldn't kill Michael. And I had his EpiPen. I took it out of his backpack. I told him all he had to do was admit what he did and he could have it."

She looked at me, waving the rock in the air. "Why didn't he just say it? Why didn't he just say the words?" She moved closer to me and I had to step back.

"What went wrong?" I asked.

She pushed her hair back off her face again. "He grabbed me. I was standing over there." She pointed to a spot on the sand.

"He was wheezing and pulling at me and I couldn't get the EpiPen and use it because he wouldn't let go, so I grabbed a rock and hit him so he would *just let go.*" The hand holding the rock now was gripping it so tightly I could see the outline of her knuckles under the skin.

She shook her head. "I'm not quite sure what I did after that, but I walked in the water that way"—she pointed in the direction opposite from Clayton Mc-Namara's property—"and eventually I got back to where I'd left my bike and I went home. I thought Michael would be fine and if he'd just done what he was supposed to do he would have been. You see that, don't you?"

I nodded. I was shaking from cold and fear. "We're both cold and wet and I'd really like to go get that coffee we talked about," I said.

"I didn't want Michael to die," Joanna said.

"I know that," I said. "Everyone will understand."

"I don't think so," she said. "I did a bad thing. I hurt my brother."

"I'll help you explain to everyone."

Joanna shook her head. "My father always said an eye for an eye and a tooth for a tooth." She raised the rock and hit herself in the temple. Then to my horror she fell sideways into the water and disappeared.

For a second I couldn't breathe. Then I managed to take a breath and then another one. I peeled off my hoodie, kicked off my shoes and jumped off the end of the breakwater feet first. The water was deep and so cold it hurt.

I came up for air, looked for Joanna and couldn't see her. I took a breath and went under again, looking for any sign of her.

Nothing.

Lungs bursting, I broke the surface, sucked in air and yelled for help. Then I took another big breath and went under again, looking and reaching through the water but I still couldn't find Joanna. I surfaced again just as I was about to pass out. Once more I hollered for help and then I dove beneath the water again, all the time repeating the same word in my head, *pleasepleasepleaseplease*.

And then my hand touched something. I grabbed at whatever it was and realized I was holding on to an arm. Joanna's arm. I kicked hard and our heads broke the surface of the water.

Joanna was unconscious. There was blood in the water around her. The jagged edge of the rock had broken her skin. I had to get her to shore. I tipped an ear to her mouth and somehow she was breathing. I wrapped my arm across her chest under her arms and swam with the other one, kicking my legs as hard as I could. A wave slapped me in the face. I coughed and sputtered, but I continued to swim.

And then I saw what I thought had to be a hallucination. Cleveland was running up the beach and out into the water faster than I had ever seen him or anyone else ever move. Once he was in chest-deep water he began swimming out to me with long, sure strokes. I continued to pull Joanna and kick and then Cleveland was there taking Joanna.

"Can you swim?" he asked. I nodded and slowly we made our way to shore, collapsing on the sand.

Cleveland bent his face to Joanna. "She's breathing," he said.

I pulled off my shirt and pressed it to the wound on Joanna's head. "She hit herself and went into the water. She killed Michael."

Cleveland shook his head.

I heard the wail of approaching sirens. It had never sounded so good.

We pulled Joanna a little higher onto the sand and I couldn't help thinking about dragging her brother's body out of the water.

The sirens got louder. Cleveland gestured at the embankment. "I'd better go show them where we are. You got this?"

I nodded. I kneeled next to Joanna and felt for her pulse with my free hand, while the other was still pressing my shirt to the side of her head. "She's still alive," I said. "I couldn't have gotten her out of the water without you."

Cleveland shrugged and gave me the faintest of smiles. "I told you if you needed me to yell," he said.

Chapter 25

The paramedics made it down the embankment with their gear. I explained what happened. Farther up the beach a police officer was talking to Cleveland, who was gesturing in my direction. I knew the officer was going to want to talk to me in a minute.

One of the paramedics took me aside and draped a blanket over my shoulders. "I need to take a look at your arm," she said.

"I'm all right," I said.

She shook her head. "You're bleeding."

I looked down to see a long gash on my right forearm.

The woman cleaned the wound, put a dressing and a bandage on it and gave me instructions on how to take care of it.

"Thank you," I said. I glanced over at Joanna. "Will she be okay?"

"I've seen a lot worse," the paramedic said. "You gave her a fighting chance."

"I'm not sure she wanted one," I said. I went to give the blanket back and the woman told me to keep it. She gave my shoulder a squeeze. "You did good. Remember that." She went to help her partner.

The police officer and Cleveland were walking in my direction and I headed toward them. The officer introduced himself and asked what happened. It turned out that Cleveland had been at the back of Clayton McNamara's property looking at an old tractor and had seen Joanna go into the water.

"Detective Andrews is going to want to know what's going on," I told the officer. I pointed at the stretcher the paramedics were carrying across the sand. "That's Joanna Norris. She killed her brother."

We finished answering questions and the police officer let us go to get into some dry things. Memphis was home. He took us both in and found me a baggy pair of sweatpants and a huge T-shirt, but it was all dry and I was very grateful.

Memphis gave me his phone to call Mac. Mine was wet and I had no idea if it would ever work again. Memphis made coffee and the three of us sat at his kitchen table.

"What were you doing out here?" Cleveland asked.

I explained about my little meltdown.

"How did Joanna Norris end up out here?" Memphis said.

I folded my hands around the oversized mug he'd given me. I wasn't sure if they were ever going to be warm again. "She was following me. I'm not sure if she was afraid she was going to get caught or afraid she wasn't."

Memphis shook his head. "I can't get my mind to go to a place where I would try to kill one of my siblings."

"That's good to hear," Cleveland said drily.

I heard voices outside and Memphis went to see what was going on.

"I'm glad you were here," I said to Cleveland. "I'm not sure I could have made it to shore with Joanna."

"You're stronger than you think," he said. "I just wish we could have saved Michael, too."

I nodded. "I know. But that's not your fault or mine." I repeated what the paramedic had said to me. "You did good. Remember that."

Saturday morning I was working in the garage on the table I was hoping to turn into a kitchen island. Mac had been out twice in about twenty minutes and the second time I had told him firmly to stop hovering, so my only company in the sunshine was Elvis, who was sitting on top of a stool watching me write down measurements on a little piece of paper.

The truck from Pine Knoll Farm pulled into the parking lot just before nine thirty. I waved and Andrew Lewis did the same. He got out and walked over to me.

"Thank you for coming," I said.

He smiled. "No problem."

Elvis meowed hello and looked Andrew over.

Andrew smiled, held out his hand and said, "Hello, puss."

"That's Elvis," I said.

The cat bumped Andrew's hand with his head and Andrew began to stroke the cat's fur.

"Joanna talked about you before she tried to kill herself," I said. Joanna was in the hospital under guard. She had pneumonia but was expected to recover. "She was—is in love with you."

Andrew nodded. "I knew that. I didn't feel the same way about her."

I had already figured that out. "She wanted to clear your name."

"I know," he said as Elvis leaned into his hand.

"Simon Kang lied about what he saw that night and Michael didn't tell anyone what *he* saw," I said.

"Joanna couldn't understand that what was done was done. I took the Alford plea. I went to jail. It was the best choice. It's over now and I just want to get on with my life now that I have it back again."

"It was the best choice," I said, "because you really did kill Freddie Black."

His eyes widened and he seemed to pull away from me just an infinitesimal degree.

"Unlike me, you're a perfect liar," I said. He looked confused, even though I knew he understood exactly what I was accusing him of. "You have no tells. If I hadn't been convinced you're a liar and a killer, nothing in your reaction would have given you away. I don't know whether to be impressed or horrified." I waited, letting the silence stretch between us.

"I didn't kill Freddie," Andrew finally said.

I looked at Elvis, who was making a sour face as though he'd just discovered he'd been tricked into a visit to the vet. "Yes, you did," I said, "although for a long time I didn't believe that. Everyone's stories from that night were so disjointed it was almost impossible to get a clear picture of what happened and when, other than that Freddie went into the water. I should have realized sooner that we were never going to be able to put together a decent timeline because pretty much everyone other than Freddie had been drinking. My second mistake was assuming that because Michael Norris saw someone else arguing with Freddie you could be innocent."

"I am innocent," Andrew said, with just the right amount of frustration in his voice.

If I hadn't been certain he was lying, and if Elvis hadn't confirmed that, I would have believed him.

"You argued just the way you said you did. And you walked away with Freddie standing on those rocks still alive."

"Just like I said I did."

I nodded. "That much of your story is true. But Freddie was argumentative. More than one person described her as prickly. And the two of you were always getting into it over something. So I'm guessing that Freddie couldn't let your argument go. And somehow you ended up on that breakwater *a second time*. But that time you hit her. You hit her hard and she went into the water and you just left her there to die." I shrugged. "I don't think you went to the party planning to kill her or maybe you did. I don't know. But I do know you made a deliberate choice to leave Freddie to die when she went in the water. You know how I know that?"

He said nothing and just stood there, his expression unreadable.

"I know," I said, "because when Joanna tried to kill herself I jumped in after her."

"You saved her life," Andrew said.

"I'm very happy I did, but I didn't think about saving Joanna's life. I didn't think about anything. I just jumped. It was instinct to try to save her. It's what makes us human. That instinct to care about each other. You didn't have that when Freddie went in the water. When she was drowning. Did you?"

Andrew looked at me for a long, silent moment. "I did my time and as far as the law is concerned the slate is clean now. I'm glad Joanna is all right." He hesitated and then added softly, "And you."

Then he walked across the parking lot, got into the truck and drove away.

I looked down at Elvis, who was vigorously washing his face. Rose stepped out from the back corner of the workroom, where she had been listening. "You were right," she said.

I shook my head. "I almost wish I wasn't."

Rose leaned down so her face was level with Elvis's. "You played your part well," she told him.

"I think that was just good luck," I said.

Elvis stopped midwash with a paw in the air and gave me an indignant look. Rose smiled. "Don't be so sure," she said.

Chapter 26

On Sunday we celebrated Avery and Greg and their graduation with a family dinner. When Rose had asked Avery how she wanted to mark her graduation this was what she said she wanted, dinner at Charlotte's house like we'd done so many times before.

"Could we invite Greg's family?" she'd asked.

"Of course," Rose had said.

Charlotte and Rose made pot roast with crispy roasted potatoes and carrots and a salad with Mr. P.'s family secret salad dressing. Greg's father and his sister and brother joined us. Nick and I surprised everyone when we got out our guitars to sing an old Johnny Rock song called "Home," which had been one of my dad's favorites. We'd only had one practice session but even I conceded that we sounded pretty good and I couldn't believe I'd let that guitar sit in the closet for so long.

Nick gave me a look, indicated the guitar and said, "Thursday?"

I opened my mouth to tell him I wasn't ready to play at the jam yet, but somehow "okay" came out instead.

After dinner I found myself standing just inside the living room watching everyone. Mr. P. was showing Greg and his father and John something on his laptop. Liz appeared to be talking about shoes with Greg's sister, Mallory. Jameis was teaching dance moves to Nick, Michelle and Greg's little brother after Jameis and Jess had wowed everyone earlier dancing to "I Hate Myself for Loving You." Charlotte, Rose and Gram were laughing over old photos with Mac. I was pretty sure some of them were embarrassing ones of me.

Jess came and leaned her head on my shoulder.

"This is my family," I said to her. "A bunch of senior citizens who investigate crimes, a sweet old man who can hack any computer system in this country, including the ones run by the government, a teenager who's either going to become an astronaut or dictator, a police detective with two left feet, a philanthropist with a shoe obsession and a best friend who, given that dance I just watched, has been holding out on me." I gestured at them all. "Look at this. This is not normal. It's wonderful, but it's not normal."

Jess laughed. "This is better than normal," she said. "This is family."

Acknowledgments

A huge thank-you to everyone at Penguin Random House who has worked with dedication and humor on putting together this book and getting the word out, especially Gabbie, Kaila, Caitlyn and Hillary. As always, thank you to my editor, Jessica Wade. Every book is better because of you. My agent, Kim Lionetti, can always be counted on to take care of a hundred little details and to give me an encouraging nudge (kick) when I need it. Thanks, Kim!

Thank you to the wonderful people in the state of Maine who make me feel welcome every time I visit. And thanks to Mike, who shared his love of cheese with me.

This book wouldn't exist without the enthusiasm of so many booksellers and readers. Thank you to everyone who has championed the Second Chance Cat Mystery series. It means more than you could know.

And last but never least, thanks to Patrick and Lauren, who always have my heart.

Love Elvis the cat?
Then meet Hercules and Owen!
Read on for an excerpt from
the first book by Sofie Kelly
in the Magical Cats Mysteries . . .

CURIOSITY THRILLED THE CAT

Available in paperback
from Berkley Prime Crime!

The body was smack in the middle of my freshly scrubbed kitchen floor. Fred the Funky Chicken, minus his head.

"Owen!" I said sharply.

Nothing.

"Owen, you little fur ball, I know you did this. Where are you?"

There was a muffled "meow" from the back door. I leaned around the cupboards. Owen was sprawled on his back in front of the screen door, a neon yellow feather sticking out of his mouth. He rolled over onto his side and looked at me with the same goofy expression I used to get from stoned students coming into the BU library.

I crouched down next to the gray-and-white tabby. "Owen, you killed Fred," I said. "That's the third chicken this week."

The cat sat up slowly and stretched. He padded over to me and put one paw on my knee. Tipping his head to one side he looked up at me with his golden eyes. I sat back against the end of the cupboard. Owen climbed onto my lap and put his two front paws on my chest. The feather was still sticking out of his mouth.

I held out my right hand. "Give me Fred's head," I said. The cat looked at me unblinkingly. "C'mon, Owen. Spit it out."

He turned his head sideways and dropped what was left of Fred the Funky Chicken's head into my hand. It was a soggy lump of cotton with that lone yellow feather stuck on the end.

"You have a problem, Owen," I told the cat. "You have a monkey on your back." I dropped what was left of the toy's head onto the floor and wiped my hand on my gray yoga pants. "Or maybe I should say you have a chicken on your back."

The cat nuzzled my chin, then laid his head against my T-shirt, closed his eyes and started to purr.

I stroked the top of his head. "That's what they all say," I told him. "You're addicted, you little fur ball, and Rebecca is your dealer."

Owen just kept on purring and ignored me. Hercules came around the corner then. "Your brother is a catnip junkie," I said to the little tuxedo cat.

Hercules climbed over my legs and sniffed the remains of Fred the Funky Chicken's head. Then he looked at Owen, rumbling like a diesel engine as I scratched the side of his head. I swear there was disdain on Hercules's furry face. Stick catnip in, on or near anything and Owen squirmed with joy. Hercules, on the other hand, was indifferent.

The stocky black-and-white cat climbed onto my lap, too. He put one white paw on my shoulder and swatted at my hair.

"Behind the ear?" I asked.

"Meow," the cat said.

I took that as a yes, and tucked the strands back behind my ear. I was used to long hair, but I'd cut mine several months ago. I was still adjusting to the change in style. At least I hadn't given in to the impulse to dye my dark brown hair blond.

"Maybe I'll ask Rebecca if she has any ideas for my hair," I said. "She's supposed to be back tonight." At the sound of Rebecca's name Owen lifted his head. He'd taken to Rebecca from the first moment he'd seen her, about two weeks after I'd brought the cats home.

Both Owen and Hercules had been feral kittens. I'd found them, or more truthfully they'd found me, about a month after I'd arrived in town. I had no idea how old they were. They were affectionate with me, but wouldn't allow anyone else to come near them, let alone touch them. That hadn't stopped Rebecca, my backyard neighbor, from trying. She'd been buying both cats little catnip toys for weeks now, but all she'd done was turn Owen into a chicken-decapitating catnip junkie. She was on vacation right now, but Owen had clearly managed to unearth a chicken from a secret stash somewhere.

I stroked the top of his head again. "Go back to sleep," I said. "You're going cold turkey . . . or maybe I should say cold chicken. I'm telling Rebecca no more catnip toys for you. You're getting lazy."

Owen put his head down again, while Hercules used his to butt my free hand. "You want some attention, too?" I asked. I scratched the spot, almost at the top of his head, where the white fur around his mouth and up the bridge of his nose gave way to black. His green eyes narrowed to slits and he began to purr, as well. The rumbling was kind of like being in the service bay of a Volkswagen dealership.

I glanced up at the clock. "Okay, you two. Let me up. It's almost time for me to go and I have to take care of the dearly departed before I do."

I'd sold my car when I'd moved to Minnesota from Boston, and because I could walk everywhere in Mayville Heights, I still hadn't bought a new one. Since I had no car, I'd spent my first few weeks in town wandering around exploring, which is how I'd stumbled on Wisteria Hill, the abandoned Henderson estate. Everett Henderson had hired me at the library.

Owen and Hercules had peered out at me from a tumble of raspberry canes and then followed me around while I explored the overgrown English country garden behind the house. I'd seen several other full-grown cats, but they'd all disappeared as soon as I got anywhere close to them. When I left, Owen and Hercules followed me down the rutted gravel driveway. Twice I'd picked them up and carried them back to the empty house, but that didn't deter them. I looked everywhere, but I couldn't find their mother. They were so small and so determined to come with me that in the end I'd brought them home.

There were whispers around town about Wisteria

Hill and the feral cats. But that didn't mean there was anything unusual about my cats. Oh no, nothing unusual at all. It didn't matter that I'd heard rumors about strange lights and ghosts. No one had lived at the estate for quite a while, but Everett refused to sell it or do anything with the property. I'd heard that he'd grown up at Wisteria Hill. Maybe that was why he didn't want to change anything.

Speaking of not wanting change, Hercules was not eager to relinquish his prime spot on my lap. But after some gentle prodding, he shook himself and got off. Owen yawned a couple of times, stretched and took twice as long to move.

I got the broom and dustpan from the porch and swept up the remains of Fred the Funky Chicken. Owen and Hercules sat in front of the refrigerator and watched. Owen made a move toward the dustpan, like he was toying with the idea of grabbing the body and making a run for it.

I glared at him. "Don't even think about it."

He sat back down, making low, grumbling meows in his throat.

I flipped open the lid of the garbage can and held the pan over the top. "Fred was a good chicken," I said solemnly. "He was a funky chicken and we'll miss him."

"Meow," Owen yowled.

I dumped what was left of the catnip toy into the garbage. "Rest in peace, Fred," I said as the lid closed.

I put the broom away, brushed the cat hair off my shirt and washed my hands. I looked in the bathroom mirror. Hercules was right. My hair did look better tucked behind my ear.

My messenger bag with a towel and canvas shoes for tai chi class was in the front closet. I set it by the door and went back through the house to make sure the cats had fresh water.

"I'm leaving," I said. But both cats had disappeared and I didn't get any answer.

I stopped to grab my keys and pick up my bag. Locking the door behind me, I headed out, down Mountain Road.

The sun was yellow-orange, low on the sky over Lake Pepin. It was a warm Minnesota evening, without the sticky humidity of Boston in late July. I shifted my bag from one shoulder to the other. I wasn't going to think about Boston. Minnesota was home now—at least for the next eighteen months or so.

The street curved in toward the center of town as I headed down the hill, and the roof of the library building came into view below. It sat on the midpoint of a curve of shoreline, protected from the water by a rock wall. The brick building had a stained-glass window that dominated one end and a copper-roofed cupola, complete with its original wrought-iron weather vane.

The Mayville Heights Free Public Library was a Carnegie library, built in 1912 with money donated by the industrialist and philanthropist Andrew Carnegie. Now it was being restored and updated to celebrate its centenary. That was why I had been in town for the last several months. And why I'd be here for the next year and a half. I was supervising the restoration—

which was almost finished—as well as updating the collections, computerizing the card catalog and setting up free internet access for the library patrons. I was slowly learning the reading history of everyone in town. It made me feel like I knew the people a little, as well.

ABOUT THE AUTHOR

Sofie Ryan is a writer and mixed-media artist who loves to repurpose things in her life and in her art. She is the author of *Fur Love or Money*, *Scaredy Cat*, and *Totally Pawstruck* in the *New York Times* bestselling Second Chance Cat Mysteries. She also writes the *New York Times* bestselling Magical Cats Mysteries under the name Sofie Kelly.

VISIT SOFIE RYAN ONLINE

SofieRyan.com